The Dreamcatcher

A DREAMLAND SERIES NOVELLA

E.J. Mellow

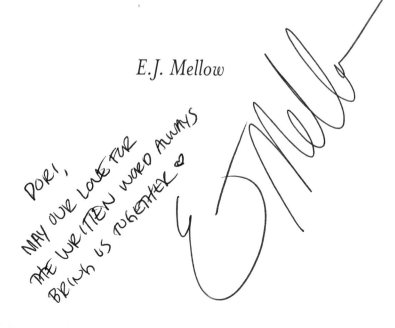

Dori,
May our love for
the written word always
bring us together ♥

The Dreamcatcher

Copyright © 2016 E.J. Mellow

Published by Four Eyed Owl, Village Station PO Box 204, New York, NY 10014

Editing & Copy Editing by Dori Harrell
Cover Design by E.J. Mellow
Cover Photography by Gabriela Slegrova Solms

ISBN: 0996211454
ISBN-13: 9780996211451

Though my soul may set in darkness, it will rise in perfect light;
I have loved the stars too fondly to be fearful of the night.

—Sarah Williams

Chapter I

THE ROOM WAS stifling with the influx of bodies packed tight, and an anxious shuffling filled the windowless space as the Nocturna guards tried to suppress their growing claustrophobia. If they felt comfortable being contained within four walls, they would have chosen a different profession. Dev cracked his knuckles one at a time, a restless habit he'd acquired after being forced to appear at these biweekly gatherings. Even though he'd graduated above the ranks of all the soldiers here, his spotty attendance was not well received.

Alex's rather verbose and overwrought reprimand of him being a role model to the rest of the cadets still rang in his ears. And it did the job to motivate him to show up so long as he never had to endure that speech again. At least the old man was effective in his irritation.

Letting out an impatient breath, Dev watched the stout general in the front of the room address the mass of soldiers. The blue-white lights above highlighted the gray in Alex's cropped hair, and his burly chest puffed up at the end of his sentences. The information he shared was always the same, or a close variation—the Metus numbers were slowly rising, extra shifts were added to the schedules of every team, and Dev and Aveline were continuously assigned to patrol the northern part of the grasslands surrounding the city.

Glancing around the white space, it was easy to discern Dev wasn't alone in his eagerness to start today's rounds. The constant twirling of Arcuses, tapping of feet, and shifting of bodies were subtle indicators for Alex to get on with it already.

"And make sure to report back every sighting or anything else odd that occurs on your patrols," the general said—his routine closing line, which was followed by its usual collection of relieved sighs.

"Thank Terra," Aveline muttered beside Dev as she stood from leaning against the wall. "I actually think I manifested the ability to sleep during that."

Dev gave his partner a wry glance. "At least that would be one positive thing that would've come from attending these things."

"Yeah, well, still not worth it." Aveline pulled her long, pale hair into a ponytail and readjusted the Arcus strap across her chest. "You ready?"

"Lead the way." He inclined his head toward the door.

Pressing tight into the cluster of other guards all waiting to exit, Dev peered down as an arm brushed against his backside. With the graze being more of a grope, he was not surprised to find thick lips fashioned into a sly smirk pointed up at him.

"Oh, sorry," the girl said in a honey-laced voice. "Close quarters." She gestured to the congested group as a way of an explanation.

"Ah yes, I forgot you have issues keeping your hands to yourself, Candice. Especially while in crowds."

"You didn't seem to think it was an issue the other night." Her gaze remained bold.

"And with you"—Dev leaned in—"I never will."

A snort came from in front of them, but he ignored it, watching as a blossom of pink spread across Candice's ebony skin. He smiled crookedly. "Safe rounds," he murmured and, with her features still in a fluster, slipped through the door.

"You're horrible," Aveline said once they'd traveled down the hall. "Why?"

"Candice has no idea what she's getting into."

"On the contrary, I think she has a very clear idea. In fact, she usually comes up with all of them. And let me tell you"—he arced a brow—"they can be pretty creatively flex—"

"*Ugh*, gag me with Metus droppings, why don't you?" Aveline shoved Dev's shoulder. "That's *not* what I meant. You shouldn't play with her like that. And yes, I realize I just set you up for another disgusting innuendo, so just don't."

A half smile flirted across his lips. "As long as you're aware."

"*Dev*," she chastened.

"Ave, she knows I don't do serious. They all know."

"Yeah, well, they have a funny way of forgetting, and then *I* have to hear about it."

"Oh, is that what this is about?" Dev turned to her, realization dawning on his face. "You don't have to be so passive aggressive. If you want me to buy you earplugs, you just have to ask."

She attempted to throw a punch to his arm again, but he sidestepped, his amused chuckle echoing down the hall.

"I give up." She stalked forward. "I'm no longer covering for you when they come to me with death threats, asking where you are."

"I like to think of those more as demands of passion." He caught up with her in two long strides.

"I pity the next girl you meet," Aveline said with a shake of her head and pushed through the doors to the outside. "I really do."

Even though Dev laughed, deep down he couldn't help but agree. The place his heart should've been had been hollowed out for decades. And though they'd all tried, desperately so, no one had yet been the one to refill it.

And Dev wasn't sure if he ever wanted to encounter anybody who could.

⋅→⟫⟩ ⟨⟪←⋅

Air whipped against his face as he careened forward, each thump of his heart a welcome reminder of the adrenaline coursing through his bloodstream. With eyes closed he imagined the same thing he always did when traveling the zipline—that he was flying, dancing across the sky like the Dreamers above, unbound by this land's gravity. His body swayed left and then right as it followed the wire around buildings, and from the many times he'd traversed this path, he knew he had ten more seconds until his grip should tighten to slow down.

"You look like an idiot when you do that," Aveline called out, causing Dev to blink his eyes open as he approached the landing where she stood.

"Takes one to know one," he said as his feet hit the platform.

Aveline snorted. "Are you sure you're older than me? Because that comeback was adolescent lame."

"That's because I have to lower them to the maturity of the people I'm around." He smiled sweetly at her.

"Right," she said with an eye roll.

"You know, Ave." Dev tilted his head to the side. "I can help you deal with it."

Her brows pinched in. "Deal with what?"

"Your overbearing love for me, of course. You obviously don't know how to deal with it, and keeping it bottled is *never* the solution." He patted her on the shoulder, and she smacked his hand away.

"You are officially delusional."

"Shh, just let it out," he cooed and then quickly pulled her into a hug "Accept the love, Ave. Feel the love."

"Colló! Dev, put me down!" She hissed as she squirmed and kicked in his arms. "I'm seriously. Going to. Murder you!"

He held steady, dodging a backward elbow to his nose, and didn't let go until she stopped struggling and went limp in defeat, just like all the other times. He grinned. "There, that wasn't so hard now, was it?" She shot him a glare that didn't quite hide the amusement in her eyes as she straightened her black T-shirt.

"I don't know how I've dealt with you over the years."

"I think you've done a fine job," he said while taking in her delicate features and skinny frame, which always brought back memories of their early days together. She was so eager to impress him when they were first partnered, to prove everyone wrong who said she was too weak, too small to be a guard. While parts of her attitude had definitely changed since then, her spark to be great had only grown into fire. Dev liked to think he had something to do with that. He made sure to teach her how to take care of herself, use her smallness as a strength, and to never fall into predictability. For in combat, as soon as one knew your tendencies, behaviors, you'd already lost.

"So do you think we'll see any tonight?" Aveline asked, gazing out to the landscape on the other side of their platform. They stood on top of the northern wall that separated the city of Terra from the rest of the land—a land that as of late had been crawling with more and more nightmares.

Stepping to her side, Dev studied the quiet field that swayed gently in the breeze below and, save for a solitary elm tree in the distance, sloped unobstructed for miles. "I don't know. They've been strangely absent the past couple rounds. Maybe if we're lucky, we will."

"Only you would think that was lucky."

His smile was coy. "What can I say? I'm a man of act—"

Dev was cut off by a bright burst of light exploding in the distant sky, and he glanced up, locking on to a burning orb falling at supersonic speed, racing to the ground. Dev shielded his eyes from the blinding light and watched with amazement as the blazing star crashed down right at the base of the elm. The ground rumbled with its contact, and the brilliant light flickered and sputtered before going dark, throwing the land once more into its usual shadow of night—as if nothing had happened at all.

"What in all of Terra?" Aveline stepped forward before looking at Dev. The shock reverberating through him was mirrored on her face, and they both remained still until a sense of duty finally registered. Like a racehorse out of the gate, Dev shot toward the grappling pole with Aveline quick on his heels, and when his feet hit the soft soil below, he lost no momentum as he turned in the direction of the fallen star and ran.

Chapter 2

GINGERLY APPROACHING THE tree, Dev scanned the area. There was no evidence that a fiery mass just fell, not even a single singed stalk or errant leaf from the tree's canopy above. The only proof of a possible disturbance was the surrounding grass being slightly bent back and a sweet scent in the air, a sign of the recent presence of Navitas.

Moving forward, Dev instantly locked on to a form, and if he thought he couldn't be any more shocked from the current events, he was very wrong. For there, lying motionless on the ground, was a girl. Her eyes were closed, and her almost black hair fanned around her head, making it appear like she was floating in water. Two pale legs protruded from funny-looking blue shorts, and long graceful arms stretched out of a plain gray T-shirt.

He glanced at Aveline before taking a couple of steps closer, and then stopped dead when the girl's eyes fluttered open. Deep pools of brown stared straight into the leaves above, and Dev couldn't help but smile when she wiggled her toes and fingers like a newborn.

"Dev," Aveline whispered. "Are you thinking what I'm thinking?"

He remained silent, too transfixed.

Could this really be happening? He wanted to gaze up at the sky, study the millions of stars zooming by like he had on so many occasions before, but he couldn't bring himself to look away.

She kept perfectly still while her eyes roamed over Aveline, assessing what was there before latching on to Dev's form. He watched in fascination as she studied him from his boots up to his head, and when their gaze connected, it was like the world rippled out from under him and then slammed back together. He stood in a frozen moment with this otherworldly stranger whose cheeks deepened in color each second he stared.

What are you thinking, little one?

Aveline's buzzing whispers snapped Dev back into the present, and with forced calm he said what they both knew. "It's a Dreamer."

Aveline sputtered in annoyance. "I see that it's a Dreamer, Dev! But what's she doing here?"

Great question, he thought as he tilted his head to the sky, watching as the stars moved across to their dreams successfully. "I'm not sure," he said. "Something must have gotten crossed with her journey to her landscape."

"That's never happened before. It's impossible," Aveline said, thumping her fists onto her hips.

Dev scratched his chin while glancing down to their newly arrived guest again. "Well, it happened now."

"Excuse me," an enticing feminine voice rang out as the girl on the ground began to sit up. She immediately stopped, however, when she caught sight of Aveline taking a protective stance. "Whoa." She raised her hands innocently, and the cute gesture had Dev taking a more detailed appraisal of the girl. Her eyes were larger than normal, saucerlike, making her emotions of annoyance and confusion easily discerned. She had light freckles dusting her delicate nose and scattered across her cheeks, drawing attention to their prominence, and her long, dark hair framed an oval face that ended with full pink lips. There was no denying her beauty.

"I'm not going to do anything but stand," she continued. "Can I stand?" She glanced back and forth between the two of them.

"She can hear us," Aveline whispered to Dev.

"Of course I can hear you! What's going on? Where am I? Who are you guys?"

Dev raised a brow while trying to bite back a smile. "Inquisitive, isn't she?"

The Dreamer let out a huff while settling back on her knees. "*Please* stop talking like I'm not right in front of you. Like I said, I can hear you. And I have a name. It's Molly."

It took all of Dev's strength not to laugh. She was simply adorable. And that name, Molly—star of the sea… He allowed another moment to admire this delightful conundrum before raising a hand to stop Aveline, who had just opened her mouth to say something they'd both most likely regret. Instead, he answered with the one thing he was probably supposed to say in a situation like this. "Hi, Molly." He stepped forward. "What's going on is that you're *dreaming*." He wiggled his fingers like the elders did when telling stories. "*Where* you are is in your dream. *Who* we are…well, we're obviously figments of your imagination."

The land fell quiet as Molly studied him, her eyes reducing to slits. "Dreaming?" she repeated.

"Yes, dreaming. You know, a series of thoughts, images, sensations occurring in a person's mind during sleep." Dev listed off part of the definition the elders made sure to hammer into them at a young age.

Molly watched the two of them from her position on the ground, her brain seeming to work in overtime, and Dev might have felt sorry for her if he wasn't too busy being captivated.

Aveline shifted for the tenth time beside him, and he wanted to tell her to hold still. He had so many questions, and the last thing he wanted was to scare the girl off. This was the first Dreamer he'd seen in the flesh, not reduced to pixels on a screen or displayed through Navitas imagery. He wasn't sure what he ever expected if given the opportunity to meet a Dreamer, but he was pretty certain Molly wasn't it.

Watching her take in their surroundings, he noted her features remained statuesque as a gentle breeze danced through her hair and sent wisps across her cheek. In the next instant her composure jilted, and her whole body stiffened as she glanced down. On a choked gasp, she threw her hands over her chest, as if realizing for the first time her attire. The mortification etched on her face pushed a chuckle out of Dev, and Molly's head snapped up to glare at him. *Oh, she's just too fun.*

"We should go." Aveline fiddled with her Arcus strap before turning to him. "Dev! Are you listening?"

"Aveline, we can't just leave her here." The thought alone made him anxious. These were the very people they lived and died to protect. How his partner could so easily abandon their sense of duty was simply lost on him, not to mention disappointing.

"And why not?" Aveline asked.

"It's not safe. We can't have her wandering around. This has never happened before, that either you or I can ever recall."

"Okay, so what do *you* suggest we do then?"

Dev brushed a hand over his head. "We need to make sure she's okay until she wakes up."

Aveline barked out a laugh. "You'd like that, wouldn't you? What even makes you think she *will* wake up? I for one don't want to waste my day sticking around to find out. We have patrols to run."

"Don't you mean night?" The Dreamer surprised him with her question.

"Excuse me?" Aveline cut a glance her way.

"Well...you said you didn't want to waste your *day*, but it's obviously night out." Molly gestured to the sky.

"Yeah, okay, *night*...whatever you say, Dreamer," Aveline scoffed, and Dev would have told his partner to stop being such a Metus spawn if he didn't see the gleam of defiance in Molly's dark gaze—a hint of a worthy adversary. Something told him she could handle Aveline just fine.

"Why do you keep calling me *Dreamer*?" Molly asked, an edge in her tone.

Ignoring Molly, Aveline faced him with a look that clearly stated her patience had run dry—not that she had much to begin with. "Okay, Dev, I've obviously lost you. I'm going to finish the rounds because *that's* what we are here to do. If you want to stay and play babysitter, be my guest."

He sighed. "This is what Tim would want us to do, Ave. You know if we left now, with her still here, and something were to happen, we would get strung out by our toes in City Hall. Aren't you in the least bit curious?"

Aveline gave a fleeting glance to Molly before turning back to him. "No."

He shook his head. "Fine, go. But I'm staying put and making sure she gets back okay."

Aveline breathed out an exasperated sigh. "All we need to do is leave and then report this to Tim. He'll take care of it."

"We can report it *after* she leaves," Dev said.

"Uh, excuse me again, guys," Molly chirped in, "but *where* am I leaving to? I still don't understand anything that's happening."

"Whatever." Aveline rolled her eyes. "I'm going. You have fun with *that*." She jerked her chin in the direction of the Dreamer and, with one last pointed look at Dev, turned to quickly make her way back to the city.

Leaving them alone.

Chapter 3

LEANING AGAINST THE elm, Dev observed Molly watching Aveline grow smaller in the distance, one of Molly's arms still draped protectively over her body as her long hair stirred softly around her face. She seemed so perfect, even in her current nervousness, and he wondered if all Dreamers were this way.

Eventually dark eyes turned to him, their deep pools twinkling the reflection of the shooting stars above, and he was momentarily unable to look away. How monotonous his days had become, how routine. Even with the slow rise of Metus, he was growing bored, listless. And he knew something would have to change fast before the past crept in, as it always did, taking up space in his seconds of rest. The appearance of this Dreamer was more than he could have hoped for.

With a frown, she blinked away from their connection and began to stand. Without thinking, and in an instant, Dev was beside her, helping. Her skin was cool and smooth, and his head swam unexpectedly as it was filled with her scent of honeysuckle and mint—a rare fragrance in these lands. Resisting the urge to lean in and graze his nose along her neck, Dev was momentarily distracted by the sight of a bandage wrapping one of her wrists.

Noticing where his attention was, Molly moved it from his view. He glanced down at her, their faces inches apart, and he suddenly became very aware of the curve of her hip, which fit seamlessly against his side.

As they remained staring, Molly shivered, and the reaction made him want to bring her into his arms—a sensation he hadn't felt in a long time.

"Are you cold?" he asked.

"Uh, no," she said, clearing her throat and moving away.

Dev watched as she fumbled with wiping debris from her clothes. "Need help?"

Her head whipped up in shock. "*No.*"

"Just trying to be polite," he said with appeasing hands raised and a crooked smile.

With a scowl, Molly concentrated on the surrounding landscape again, and Dev wondered if this experience wasn't that strange for her, given that she dreamt something different every night. Would this end up being just another imagined story, lost and forgotten among her many? The thought put weight on his chest.

"So where are we?" Molly asked, glancing over her shoulder.

"We're in your dream," he replied automatically.

"Really?" She lifted a brow. "Then who are you? I've never seen you before. So how am I recalling you here?"

"Isn't it obvious?" Dev asked, gesturing to himself. "I'm the man of your dreams."

Her eyes bulged, and Dev pressed his lips together to stifle a laugh. *She's too easy.*

"I highly doubt that," Molly bit out and looked away. After running a frustrating hand through her hair, she stomped forward.

"Where are you going?" Dev was quick to catch up to her.

"Oh, so you're allowed to ask questions, but I'm not?"

"If I recall correctly, you've asked questions."

"Yeah, none of which you've answered truthfully." She made a sharp turn away from him, but Dev's speed rivaled hers, and in a flash he walked backward in front of her.

"Why do you think I haven't answered truthfully?" he asked.

"Because I don't dream."

Dev stopped dead, and Molly faltered to keep herself from running into him. "What did you say?" He frowned down at her.

"I said, I don't dream. Well not really, not like this." She motioned around them.

"You don't *dream*?" he asked, more so he could hear it from his own lips. A Dreamer who didn't dream…it made no sense.

"Uh…not really. I mean, we all dream, I guess, right? At least that's what they say. I can never remember them when I wake up though. I don't know. I've just never felt so awake in a dream before. Like right now, I find it impossible that I could be sleeping when… when I can feel and smell and see so much." On that, Molly closed her eyes while taking in a deep breath, and Dev took in the wave of calm that settled around her. She was even more startlingly beautiful like this, and when her eyes slowly opened to lock on to his, Dev knew in that instant he was in trouble. "Yeah, well, you get what I mean." She struggled to meet his gaze, tucking a strand of hair behind one ear.

Who was this girl? Dev thought. Why did she come here? For everything that happened in Terra had a purpose, a reason for existing. Molly showing up couldn't have been a random mistake.

"You do realize people consider staring to be rude," Molly eventually said with a frown, and Dev watched as her cheeks flushed redder the longer he kept his attention on her. Knowing he was the cause slipped a smile onto his face.

"Am I making you uncomfortable?" he asked.

Her chin tipped up, and her mouth popped open to respond, but no words came out. They seemed stuck in her throat as her wide, unblinking eyes became lost in their gaze, and though she was looking straight at him, she seemed in a whole other place, a different time. That's when he smelled the sweet scent of Navitas, and like a mirage forming in the desert, their surroundings changed to reveal a blazing hot sun illuminating down on a tropical island, where they stood. Salty air pushed against his back and through his T-shirt as the sound of waves hitting a shore encircled them, the night of Terra a distant ring.

On a gasp, Dev took startling steps back, absorbing the quickly manifested illusion—an illusion that crunched under his boots and warmed his skin. *In all of Terra…* Tipping his head back, he almost burst into tears to find a blue sky orbiting their newly created oasis. And though his eyes squinted at the unfamiliar introduction of daylight, he stared and stared and stared at the sun until they watered and ached at the back of his skull. That's when he found himself dropping to the sand and stretching out, forgetting entirely whom he was with and where they were supposed to be. This was simply amazing, beyond anything he ever thought could exist on the other side of Terra's dimensional barriers. Sure, they had places with manifestations of beaches, but this...this was pure from the source. With the new sensation of heat on his skin, he smiled wide, imagining what it must be like to be human, to live your days when the sun rose and sleep when it set. His grin grew wistful. He had no idea how long this would last, but he knew without a doubt who created it.

"What are you doing?" Molly's amused voice floated over to him, and he twisted in the sand as she took a seat beside him.

"What are you thinking about?" he asked, and she blinked as if his question caught her off guard.

"What do you mean?"

"What were you thinking about a couple moments ago? When we were in the field?"

"Uh...nothing. I can't remember," she said too quickly and bit her bottom lip. Though he could tell she was holding something back, Dev didn't press the matter, his own hypothesis taking shape for how this island could have been created. He studied the way the sun softly brushed along her skin and deepened the freckles already peppered across her nose. This was how she looked to most, glowing under the light of day, and he hungered to take in every detail.

Digging his fingers into the sand beside him, he hit up against something solid. Glancing down, he found the tip of a shell peeking out of the grains and plucked it up, tracing the spiral design to its center. Terra's beaches didn't have shells, but he'd seen them in pictures. This was another reminder that what they made in Terra was a mere imitation of the real thing. He wondered what else the ecosystem engineers left out in their creations to mimic Earth and if they did it consciously or not.

"That's a good find," Molly said, looking at what he held in his hand. "You usually don't get one completely intact like that."

Dev peered up at her, fascinated by the way her hair glittered red under the sun. "Yes," he said, no longer thinking about the shell. "It is a good find."

Under his unrelenting gaze, the color on her cheeks deepened again, and she turned away to stare at the shallow sea surrounding them. A lazy smile slipped onto Dev's lips as he did the same, picking up where the water ended and the familiar dark field in the distance began.

For once, Dev's mind was clear of any unwanted thoughts, a calm settling over him that he hadn't felt since...well, since almost forever. Eventually, a movement out of the corner of his eye brought his attention back to Molly, who was playing with the bandage on her wrist.

"What happened?" Dev asked as he gently brought her arm to him, but all too quickly she pulled it back.

"I have a burn," she said.

"A burn?" Dev drew his brows together. "Did you do it to yourself?"

"Oh no! Nothing like that."

"Like what, then?"

"You'd never believe me if I told you."

"Try me."

Her soft laughter flowed over him. "Okay, I got struck by lightning."

Dev sat up straighter. "Right now? Before you came here?"

"No, and I guess yes…a couple of days ago. Why?"

He didn't respond at first, too busy shifting through a multitude of rapid thoughts and wondering if the lightning had rewired her dream travel. After all, it was Terra's symbol for their kinship with Earth. They were taught in their youth that the same energy they needed to survive, the Navitas, was also found in the lightning that flashed during human storms. It was Terra's dimensional connection bursting through into Earth's atmosphere, the only hint of the existence of their world. "But that doesn't explain your wrist being bandaged," Dev said, glancing back to the subject in question.

"I was wearing jewelry, and it burned me when I got hit." She lightly touched the white material. Dev watched the gentle movement, continuing to spin the seashell between his fingers.

"So does this kind of thing happen often?" Molly asked, nodding to their surroundings.

Taking in the crashing of the waves hitting the shoreline and the sea air mixing with the sun's rays, Dev glanced to her. "No…I wouldn't say that it does."

"Well, I really hope I don't forget this dream."

Hearing Molly's words sent an urge flooding through him to tell her the truth, that this wasn't all a dream. For Dev strangely didn't want her to forget either, but he remained silent, instinctively knowing he shouldn't mention any more about this place. He was probably interfering already by talking to her. If she was meant to come back, she'd come back. Dev definitely had no say in the matter, learning the hard way that fate held the cards with things like this.

"What's happening?" Molly's anxious voice brought him out of his thoughts, and he watched her helplessly search around her legs, as if something were touching them.

But there was nothing, only air, and Dev frowned, knowing the cause. "You're waking up."

"Waking up?" Molly's panicked eyes found his, her words suddenly sent away in a hasty breeze. Then it all happened quickly—on the sound of her next gasp, she vanished, taking the illusion she created with her.

Dev was left leaning in the cold grass, the brightness instantly blinking to darkness, the field once again back in its place and painted in night. Breathing deep, he attempted to settle an ache blossoming in his chest, desperate to catch any last gust of sea air or honeysuckle fragrance. Anything to prove she was just there.

But there was nothing, only the scent of midnight dew and the rhythmic buzz of insects in the grass.

Frustrated, Dev balled his hands into fists, instantly loosening one as he felt a solid object in his palm. Glancing down, he was surprised to find the seashell he twirled only moments ago, its white surface now a dull gray with the absence of sun. He turned it over, tracing the spiral design again. Why did this remain?

His heart picked up, and he lifted his head to gaze at the shooting stars above, searching for any that might burn brighter than the rest, as a sudden certainty began to mix in with all his confusion.

She would return, he thought, grasping the shell more firmly. He knew she would return. What he didn't know was whether he could handle the next thing she'd leave behind.

Chapter 4

THE SLURPING GREW louder, and Dev wiped away an errant splatter of sauce when it hit his cheek. "You know, I'm pretty sure you're meant to chew that," he said, cocking a brow at his large friend across the table. Rae twirled more spaghetti onto his fork while simultaneously shoving a meatball into his mouth with another.

"I chew," Rae said once he swallowed the ball whole.

"From the splatter stains covering the table and myself, I contest that statement."

"Well, I have to suck them up first," he mumbled through a new mouthful of food. "Only way to get those slippery guys in there."

Sitting in their favorite restaurant, Dev lazily skimmed over the small intimate establishment located on the second floor of Anima—a biodome of Earth's ecosystems, where Terra agriculturists harvested a majority of the food. Anima was an imposing, mostly glass structure that took up a large section in the center of the city and was frequented by the Nocturna, for it was the only place one could find sunlight in their world. Even if it was a replica of the real thing, it was better than the alternative their lives only allowed them.

Dev's attention returned to Rae, and he watched with awed terror as his companion began folding spaghetti between slices of bread. They had been coming to Elario's since they first met a decade ago at a security summit, and while Dev could never quite match Rae's gusto for sustenance, he could certainly appreciate a fine meal when he came across it—and Elario's was the best. It was reviewed by the Vigil as an exact match in quality, if not better, of the food often found in Earth's small Italian towns, so it was no shock that it had become a coveted spot.

Quickly leaning back, Dev barely missed getting hit with another spray of sauce, marveling at how none of it made its way onto his friend. Rae's dark skin and blond hair remained clean despite his aggressive efforts to consume his meal as rapidly as possible. "So what do you think?" Dev asked, bringing their conversation back to its original topic.

"About which part?" Rae didn't look up as he ate another forkful.

"About her being sent for a reason."

"I think we can find meaning in all things," Rae said while motioning to a passing waiter for more wine.

"How can you be so calm about this?" Dev said once the server left. "A Dreamer—the very ones *you* go out every day to protect, came *here*. Don't you want to know why?"

"Of course, but sometimes it's best not to jump straight into action."

"So you think I have no basis for believing it wasn't more than some random fluke that brought her here?"

Rae took a sip of his drink, and his controlled demeanor caused Dev to grind his teeth together. Rae hadn't reacted the way Dev assumed he would. It was unheard of, if not impossible, for a human to break through into their dimension. How could the same man who almost punched a garbage can when finding out his favorite ice cream shop closed be so nonchalant about this? It didn't make sense.

"I think we'll need to wait and see if she comes back to decide that," Rae said, taking his time putting down his glass.

"And if she does..."

"Then yeah, I'd say there's a reason for it."

Dev exhaled a long breath and glanced around the dimly lit space. Mostly Nocturna filled the restaurant, preferring it to other Anima eateries, not only because of the quality but also because one side had a floor-to-ceiling glass wall, allowing the patrons a replica view of a lazy afternoon Tuscan landscape, or at least what they thought it looked like. Roving honey-colored hills swayed in the distance, and even though they were separated from the carefully monitored ecosystem, Dev could almost feel the warmth radiating through from the other side. The sensation brought up phantom memories of his last encounter with the sun.

"And you said she just...fell from the sky?" Rae asked, turning Dev's attention back to him.

"Yeah, a star separated from the rest and crashed down. Then"—he flicked his hand out—"she was there."

"Hunh." Rae frowned, his gaze momentarily unfocused.

"What?"

Rae blinked his eyes back to clarity. "Nothing. Just trying to get the events straight."

Dev leaned in, lowering his voice. "I'm telling you, if you saw the beach, how detailed everything was, there's no denying she created it. I mean, the Navitas *does* come from them. There has to be a purpose for her showing up here."

"Maybe that was it—giving you a little dose of a Dreamer's vacation destination was her purpose."

Dev shot his friend a petulant glare. "I'm being serious."

Rae dropped his bread roll and leaned back, finally giving Dev his undivided attention. "All right, so if she has been sent for some reason, what are you going to do about it? What *can* you do?"

Dev scratched the back of his neck. This was the same question he'd been spinning through his mind since she left. "I don't know yet, but...there has to be something."

"Something," Rae repeated. "Yeah, real solid plan. Definitely do something."

Dev pursed his lips. "I obviously haven't figured it all out yet. I need more time with her to make sense of things."

"And you think she's definitely coming back?"

"Yes," Dev said without a hesitation.

Rae rubbed his lips together. "You have to be careful with this one, Dev. If she comes to you again, you have to be cautious of what you tell her."

Dev picked at the tablecloth. "I know."

"Do you? Because this...development, if it happens again, will need to be reported to the elders. *I'll* have to report it, and I don't want you to get in trouble for not going to them first."

"I told Tim and Alex as soon as I came back."

"Yeah." Rae nodded. "And thankfully that's all you told."

Dev frowned. "What do you mean?"

Before Rae could respond, Aveline stomped over to their table.

"How in all of Terra are you guys still eating?" she asked before waving off her friends hovering by the entrance of the restaurant. "Don't you usually finish your meal as soon as it hits the table?" She pointedly looked at Rae while he delicately refolded his napkin.

"The first three, yes. Meal four and five are meant to be savored."

She snorted a laugh. "You do know humans think gluttony is a sin, right?"

"Then it's lucky for me that I'm not human." As if to prove his point, Rae snagged a chocolate tart from a dessert cart as it was wheeled by.

Aveline rolled her eyes and took a seat. "We have to leave, Dev."

"I'm aware," he said while glancing distractedly out the glass window, his pulse quickening in anticipation for their rounds—a feeling of excitement that he had thought was lost to him.

"You're thinking about her again, aren't you?"

Dev found her calculated gaze. "And if I am?"

"Why are you so obsessed?" She turned to Rae. "Has he been bleeding your ears about this *sent for a reason* nonsense as well?"

Rae raised his brows while glancing between the two of them, clearly knowing full well to remain silent.

"We really can't get preoccupied by this," Aveline continued to Dev. "You always told me past shifts can't distract from the next shifts. That's how mistakes happen."

"Aveline," Dev said impatiently, "this wasn't any old run-in with the Metus. This was a *Dreamer*."

"All right, let's keep it down a bit." Rae flickered his gaze around the busy establishment.

Dev took in a calming breath. "I really don't understand how either of you can be writing this off so easily. I mean, you wanted to leave her there, for Terra's sake." He pinned Aveline with a look. "That goes against everything taught to us in training. We serve to protect. Serve to guard—"

"Serve to honor our creation. Yes, I know our pillars of belief, Dev."

"You didn't seem to yesterday."

Aveline rubbed her forehead. "It's just that…well, I don't trust her showing up the way she did."

"What do you mean?" Dev asked.

"It seems so random, yet way too convenient."

"You do realize that's a bit of a contradiction," Rae pointed out.

"Never mind." Aveline waved a dismissive hand.

"No, explain," Dev pushed. "What do you mean, too convenient?"

"I don't know. Just that she happened to come here *right* when we got to the platform and landed *right* where we usually start our patrols."

"Exactly." He sat up straighter, his sense of determination stirring again. "Can't you see why I'd want to know more? Why this seems serendipitous?"

"Or like a trap," Aveline countered.

Dev rested against the back of his chair, a smile inching along the side of his mouth. "When did you become such a skeptic?"

"Around the same time a girl's kept your interest longer than a few hours."

Rae choked on a sip of wine while simultaneously letting out a splutter of laughter.

Dev raised a brow at the two. "I don't know what you're implying."

"That this behavior isn't like you."

"And?"

"And it makes me worried."

Dev chuckled. "Ave, if there's one thing you never have to do, it's worry about me."

She shook her head. "I just think this should be handled at arm's length. Let the Vigil take care of it if she comes back. I would think this would fall under their jurisdiction anyway. She *is* a human, after all," Aveline said in a hushed voice. "This seems like something that should be dealt with carefully."

"That's what I told him," Rae said, popping a toothpick.

"Because it's good advice." Aveline nodded.

"Guys, really." Dev rolled his eyes. "You can take a breath. It's me here. When have I ever not been careful?"

His companions stared at him for a beat.

"Um, maybe the time you thought it would be fun to sneak into a Metus den," Aveline said pointedly.

"Or when you became convinced you could walk the zipline like a tightrope," Rae added.

"All right." He held up a hand. "I get it. But this is different. This is a Dreamer. She's not a threat."

"How can you be so sure?" Aveline asked.

"Trust me." Dev laughed. "If you had hung around longer, you'd understand. There's no way. What could she possibly do to me?"

Even though his question was meant to be rhetoric, the anxious glances shared between his two friends seemed to fill the heavy silence with many different answers.

Chapter 5

DEV FLEXED HIS fingers before squeezing his hand into a fist over and over, as if that could relieve the tension he still felt from the images that clung to his retinas like a spot left after the flash of a bulb. The recent memory of long, smooth legs that disappeared into barely there shorts was testing his strength as a man. Not to mention walking away from slipping one of the delicate straps from her shoulders pushed the limits of him remaining a gentleman, though some might argue that never actually existed.

On either side of him the harsh whispers of Tim and Aveline filled the apartment as they sat around the dining table, each of his flatmates trying to discuss as much as possible during the tight window of time before Molly returned. The fireplace crackled in the background, and its pinkish glow mixed with the low blue-white lights around the room, layering the space in a warm pastel hue. Even in the dimness, Dev knew the moment she left the bathroom to make her way through the shadowed hallway back into the living room. She had pulled her hair up into a ponytail, and the change caused her features of large eyes, prominent cheekbones, and full lips to be even more startling.

Dev had been in the midst of making his way to the northern field in anticipation for her arrival, when he caught sight of a form traveling toward their apartment. But it wasn't her unexpected appearance in the city that had Dev clenching his jaw in silent frustration—it was what he saw when he took in the rest of her. Aveline's borrowed clothes clung to every curve, the dip of her waist, and he didn't know which outfit he preferred more—the washcloth-sized clothes she arrived in or this practically painted-on ensemble she wore now.

Molly took a seat beside him, and he hadn't realized the room had grown quiet until Tim spoke.

"If I didn't know better, I would have thought you belonged here, Molly. Those clothes suit you very nicely."

"Really?" She grimaced, looking down at herself. "I feel kind of ridiculous in them, to be honest. I don't normally wear anything like this."

"Obviously," Aveline said under her breath, and Dev couldn't help chuckling at the reactionary glare Molly gave her. Seemingly annoyed at being at the expense of his amusement too, she straightened and turned to Tim.

"So, Timon, that's an interesting name. I've never heard it before."

"Yes, it's not that common." He gave her an easy smile. "It's a biblical name and means wisdom. Everyone's name has a meaning. *Aveline*, for example"—he motioned toward her—"means life. While Dev"—he placed a hand on Dev's shoulder, who winced, knowing what was coming—"is short for *Devlin*, of Irish origin, and means fierce courage."

Aveline giggled next to Dev, and he shot her a scowl.

"What?" Molly asked, glancing between the three of them.

"*Devlin* thinks his name sounds feminine." Aveline smirked.

"Shut up." He shoved her shoulder, which only made her laugh more, and Dev had to refrain from going over and putting his full weight on her. It was an immature cheap maneuver but almost always affective in winning their arguments.

"So, Molly." Tim routed the conversation back to him. "Where you come from, you have a last name as well. What is it?"

Her brows drew together. "Spero, uh, my last name is Spero."

The room went quiet as a chill ran down Dev's spine.

"What?" Molly frowned. "What is it? Does it mean something bad?"

Tim recovered first with a clearing of his throat. "Molly, which originates from Mary, can mean star of the sea. And Spero...Spero means hope. So your full name can translate to mean—"

"Star of Hope," Dev said softly, his gaze unable to leave the Dreamer, wondering what other surprises lay hidden away.

When he mentioned to Aveline the idea that Molly might have been sent to help with the Metus, she had laughed so hard he thought she might choke on the sandwich she was eating. It was a good thing she didn't, because in that moment Dev was undecided if he would have helped her.

But now, with Molly's name meaning what it did, how could his friends possibly deny there being a reason for her presence? Dev studied Molly's soft hands, the way her thin arms stretched out of her black T-shirt, not a sign of rigorous training anywhere. How much of her strength resided from within and how much would be required to manifest on the outside?

"Star of Hope. Okay...so?" Molly glanced to each of them. "Why are you guys looking at me like that?" She tucked a lock of hair behind her ear. "It's just a name."

"You must excuse us." Tim leaned into her. "Here, names have great meaning and importance. It's sort of prophetic for what one will be capable of accomplishing."

Her eyes sparked on something he said, before they narrowed. "Where is *here?*"

Tim smiled smoothly before patting her on the back. "We'll just have to see, won't we?"

Molly's shoulders slumped. "What does that even mean?" she asked and, when no one answered, dropped her head into her hands and sighed. The childish action caused Dev to smile.

Abruptly her head whipped up, her gaze searching for his, and when it connected, he worked hard to keep himself composed, the depths in her dark eyes threatening for him to fall in. "Dev, you said out on the fire escape that you liked what I was wearing tonight better than what I was wearing last night..."

A smirk lifted his lips. "You liked that, huh."

"No," Molly said with an eye roll, "I mean, you said you saw me *last night.*"

Under the table, Dev's hand tightened on his thigh, but he otherwise kept his features relaxed, even coy. "Did I say that?"

"You just admitted you did. You *also* said to Tim that I'm the wonder you were telling him about. If we've never met, how could you talk about me?"

Colló. He needed to remember how observant she was. The silence that settled around them was thick, dramatizing the soft snap of the fire in the background. Keeping his stare steady, Dev refused to look away first and admit she was right. But by the small grin that formed at the corner of her mouth, he realized, with annoyance, that she already thought she was.

"I know you two would love to stare into each other's eyes all day." Aveline cut through the tension by pushing him in the shoulder. "But we have rounds to make, Dev."

He held Molly's gaze a moment longer, her determined concentration slowly melting his aggravation into amusement. With a flash of a smile, he stood.

"That's it?" She gaped. "You're not going to explain yourself?"

"I have nothing to explain," he said passively as he headed to their gear closet, feeling Molly's glare stabbing him in the back the whole way. He'd rather deal with her anger than with getting in trouble for telling her the truth. He couldn't mess up his chances to be allowed around her. There were still too many questions, and he needed time with her to test some of his theories.

Removing his equipment from the Navitas charging stations, he swung the holder onto his back and let the Arcus drop into its chamber, hearing the top close over with an audible snap. Turning back around, he caught Molly watching him with fascination rather than annoyance.

"All right, Tim, we'll catch you later," Aveline said from the front door, waiting for Dev to follow.

He didn't move. Instead he kept his attention on Molly. "Well, aren't you coming?" he asked.

"Uh, what?" Aveline's sharp tone knocked into him. "She is so *not* coming with us!"

"Of course she is," Dev said simply. There was no way he was letting the Dreamer out of his sight. As far as he was concerned, as long as Molly was in Terra, he'd be with her. The meaning of her name tumbled around his mind again.

Aveline growled as she pointed to Dev while looking at Tim. "See this, Tim? *See!* This is exactly what I was talking about! He's lost his mind."

"I resent that statement," Dev said while leaning against the wall and studying his nails.

Aveline took in a deep breath. "Dev," she began tightly, "please explain to me why Molly needs to come with us?"

He shrugged. "Because it would be fun."

"Fun," she repeated.

"Yes, fun."

"So it would be *fun*, not dangerous and probably illegal, and the stupidest idea anyone has ever had in the entire existence of mankind?"

"Nope. Just fun." Pushing off the wall, he strode over to Molly, who took in his approach with wide eyes, her apprehension clearly apparent.

"It's okay. I don't mind staying with Tim," she said.

"You're coming with us." Hooking his hand under her arm, he pulled her to her feet.

"Are you sure this is a good idea?" Tim asked, his fingers combing through his graying beard.

"I think it's one of the best ideas I've ever had." Dev walked toward the door with Molly in tow, and made a point not to glance Aveline's way. He'd worked with her long enough to know the scowl that would paint her features. Swinging the front door open, he turned to Molly. "Ladies first."

She took in the awaiting exit and then him, a far-away look momentarily coating her gaze before an expectantly radiant smile lit up her face. Dev's breath hitched. *In all of Terra*, she was beautiful. Molly blinked as he grinned back, her features sobering as she retreated a step.

"I wasn't smiling at you," she said pointedly.

"I see." Dev looked around with raised brows. "So it was for the other man who opened the door for you?"

"As a matter of fact, it was," Molly said and breezed past him.

Though her answer had him frowning, the way her honeysuckle fragrance brushed by him in a tantalizing trail made it impossible not to turn his head and follow. Stepping into the hallway, he was immediately transfixed by the curve of her darkened silhouette and the hypnotic sway of her hips. The vision of her radiant smile surrounded him, and he felt a crack in his meticulously constructed plan to be careful. A crack that formed from the presence of too bright a light of a fallen star.

Chapter 6

THE SEASHELL DANCED rhythmically through his fingers as he waited under the tree's canopy. A soft breeze flirted through the field, and the tall grass bent away from its touch, teasing it to try again. Dev's gaze roved the still night, his senses tuning in and out to the different stimulations of the land—the bright lights zipping above, the buzzing of insects below, and the hushed rustle of leaves around him.

These quiet moments were a luxury. They were also a curse. For thoughts liked to fill silences such as these, and memories tended to live there. Dev's time limit to keep both at bay was running out, so when he smelled the delicate collection of Navitas in the air, he let out a relieving sigh. She was coming.

Like a hiccup in the folds of space, the area directly in front of him warped slightly before a soft light blurred his vision. In an instant it all disappeared, leaving a new form on the cool ground.

Dev studied her as she lay on her back, eyes closed. She wasn't wearing the same thing that she came in last night, and he felt a slight dip of disappointment. A dark jacket was thrown over a loose-fitting shirt, and tight jeans encased her toned legs. He tilted his head to the side. Okay, the jeans he liked.

Rolling over, a distressed mewl emanated out of Molly, and Dev pushed up from the tree, a slight panic setting in. *Was she hurt?* But when she sloppily swatted at nothing, her eyes opening with a grimace, he relaxed, for she was suffering from an ailment all of her own making.

He was never a big drinker, even during the darker times, but he'd helped enough comrades home after long hours spent trying to forget a recent horror to know when someone had overindulged.

He watched in fascination as Molly, with great effort, crawled her way to lean against the tree, still unaware of his presence beside it. Once she was settled and looked almost peaceful, he stepped forward.

"Had a little too much fun?"

She jumped, letting out a squeak of surprise. "Please *stop* doing that." She groaned, grabbing her stomach.

He couldn't hide his smile. "What's the celebration?" he asked, taking a seat beside her.

"Being a Saturday," she mumbled and hid her face in her hands, her long, dark hair tumbling around her shoulders.

He slid his gaze over her form again, not realizing he was looking for a peek of her soft skin. This was the most covered up she'd ever been. "I think I like what you normally sleep in compared to this." He plucked at her blazer.

"I think that should offend me, but I feel too horrible to care at the moment."

He chuckled and found himself fighting an urge to tuck a strand of her hair behind her ear so he could see her face. He balled his hands into fists instead.

"Dev?" Molly said his name with a slow lift of her head.

He could listen to her say his name for days.

"Yes, Molly?"

"Why do I still feel drunk here if I'm supposed to be dreaming?"

He shook his head in amusement—just arrived and already asking questions. No wonder the Vigil elders summoned him before coming here. None reacted with much surprise when he officially reported a Dreamer had broken into Terra, but Dev hadn't really expected anything different. The elders were a strange group of cryptic tongues and hidden emotions. No one knew if their ability to appear apathetic was a trait given to them during creation or learned in their rigorous secret studies. Whatever the cause, Dev was unconcerned at the moment, for apart from barely batting an eye when he finished his report, their only instructions were to not tell her any specifics about Terra or himself. He left promptly after that, conceding to their demands and not asking anything further in case they changed their minds and ordered him to stay away. Not like that would have stopped him, but it was best to follow the rules when possible, especially if they didn't really interfere with his plans.

"Well, your mind here is the same mind you've got when you're awake," he said with a scratch of his chin. "So if your brain is still drunk right before you go to sleep, why wouldn't it stay that way when you're asleep?"

"So I guess that means I really am dreaming. None of this is real?" She motioned to their surroundings.

He smirked. "It would seem so, wouldn't it?"

With a sigh, she turned away, and Dev decided this was as good a time as any for a distraction. Standing, he extended his hand to her. "Come on. I want to show you something."

As he helped her up, she wobbled slightly on her feet and grabbed his arm for purchase. It took a second to realize her grip on him, and he glanced down at her, a huge grin plastering across his face. "Molly…are you feeling my muscle?"

As if she'd been slapped, she whipped her hand away, eyes wide in mortification. "What? No!"

"I mean, you're welcome to feel them?" He playfully flexed his bicep and tilted it toward her.

"Just…shut up." She pushed at his arm, and he couldn't help laughing again. This was too good. "Actually, you know what? I don't think I'm in the mood to see whatever it is you want to show me after all." She turned and stormed away.

Dev reached out and twirled her back in the direction he wanted them to go.

She squeaked and shoved out of his hold. "I'd rather not be manhandled."

In all of Terra, she was making this too easy for him. "So you think I'm a man?"

"Gah!" She threw her hands up in exasperation. "Whatever. Let's go see what's so great."

With a hidden smile, Dev followed behind her retreating form.

Molly groaned as she pulled her heeled boot out of the soft ground, a repeated issue that forced them to walk at an unproductive pace.

She studied the mud now concealing the majority of the soft suede, and with a resigned sigh tried balancing on one leg to remove them. Dev extended a hand to help, and she grabbed on to him without question. With her fingers interlocking with his, he became momentarily fascinated by it. He had forgotten what it was like to be connected like this, and the feeling was both foreign and familiar. He didn't know if it was because of the girl or the years of denying himself such intimacy, but whatever the cause, it felt right. As soon as Molly became barefoot, they silently pressed on, and it wasn't until they neared their destination that Dev realized he had never let go.

And she hadn't asked him to.

Chapter 7

HER FIGURE WAS a black outline set against a darker expanse, and her hair danced in the wind as she gazed out from the canyon's lip. Dev had been indecisive about showing her this place, not knowing if it was going against the elders' rules, but he couldn't see how it would hurt. Nothing about the Edge would give away that this place was anything more than a dream. Terra ran for miles in every direction, but in all the years he'd been alive, he knew of no one who had traveled beyond this deep carved-out separation to the east. Having been nicknamed the Edge seemed more than fitting.

"This is amazing," Molly said, her hushed voice drifting to him on the wind.

"I come here every so often," Dev said, settling on a nearby rock. "It's strangely humbling to look at something bigger than yourself."

She was quiet for a moment, then said, "I've wondered what was beyond the field—if it kept on going." She glanced over her shoulder, brown eyes meeting his, and he patted the space beside him.

Taking a seat, she removed her blazer, the movement causing her fragrance to encircle him, and his eyes briefly closed.

"So," she said, shifting slightly, "do you think you'll ever explain why you always know when I'm here?"

Dev held back a grin. "One day, if you're lucky, I'll show you."

"What does that even mean?" she groaned.

"You'll understand when the time's right." Would the elders ever let him speak the truth?

"Well, can you at least give me a straight answer about something when I'm awake?"

Dev eyed her from the side. "I can try."

"Why can't I remember you when I wake up?"

A pain hit him low in his chest, and he worked to control his expression. *Why can't I remember you?* Standing, he walked to the ledge, letting the blackness of the ravine's bottom swallow up his confused emotions. Why did that bother him? It shouldn't have.

It couldn't.

Squaring his shoulders, he took in a calming breath. "Your brain is completely closed off when you sleep, only concentrating on resting. So it's easier for you to remember me here than out there." He gestured to the space in front of them. "When you wake up, you have a lot more to think about, so the things that happen while you sleep get pushed to the back of your mind."

The sound of her bare feet against the pebbled ground announced her approach. "So will I remember that you just told me this?" she asked, coming to stand by his side.

Dev peered down at her. "I'm not really sure. I'm still trying to figure out how much you'll remember."

"Why? What else is there to tell me?" A sudden breeze whipped a strand of her hair across her face, and he turned, tucking it behind her ear. "There's nothing else. I'm not sure why I said those things. You must be making them up for me to say."

She bit her bottom lip, her frustration evident. If she truly didn't remember this place when she awoke—didn't remember him—would it really matter if she heard the truth? Would it ease the bit of pain he saw swimming in her eyes? He had a strong urge to tell her everything.

"Mols…" Her name escaped his lips like the ache he felt inside, and he noticed she shivered. "Are you cold?" he asked, running a finger along her prickled arm. She shook her head, seeming incapable of words. "If it makes you feel any better, I never forget *you* when you leave."

Her mouth parted as if to respond, but instead she took in a stuttered breath and swallowed. Dev studied the movement in her neck, trailing his gaze down her soft skin until it disappeared under her silk top. *What was she doing to him?* He couldn't help it when he found himself moving closer, resigning the responsibility of whatever happened next.

"Molly, I can't explain it, but there's something about you that makes me know this is all happening for a reason." His attention stayed pinned to her. "You're my hope," he finished softly, his body swaying forward, a pull to be closer to her burning throughout him. This same desire also had warning bells sounding, telling him to move away, remove himself from her intoxicating scent and unknown mind. Something about her threatened to shake the foundation of his carefully constructed walls, and he knew this woman was the last thing he should allow to crumble them.

Like a soft caress, an orange light crept across Molly's cheek, coating the side of her face with warmth, and with an acute awareness, Dev blinked to clarity. Quickly turning, he searched the landscape and cursed as a fiery haze lifted off the horizon. Such a scene could pass as the beginning of a peaceful sunrise, but he knew there was only one thing that brought forth such a glow—the Metus.

"What is it?" Molly asked, and he spun back to her, momentarily forgetting she was there.

Colló. This wasn't good.

"You have to wake up now," he said, and when she didn't respond, he grabbed her shoulders. "Listen, you have to wake up. I have to go."

She glanced from the light in the distance back to him. "I'll go with you."

He would've laughed under different circumstances. "No." He shook his head. "That's not an option."

"Well, I'm not staying here."

"I know. You're going to wake up."

Her eyes sparked with defiance. "How? You can't make me."

Wrong thing to say.

A challenge was like a siren's call to Dev, and now it potently mixed with the adrenaline already pumping in his veins to get Molly out of here and safely awake. Glancing to the ravine behind her, a small smile inched across his lips. It would have to do, he thought, for there was no time to come up with other options. Taking predatory steps forward, Molly followed with ones back, now regarding him with uncertainty.

"Dev?"

"I'm extremely sorry, but it's for your own good."

"What is?" Molly asked, her eyes darting behind her as her heels came close to dangling over the lip.

"This."

And then Dev shoved her into the abyss.

→─══◉ ◉══─←

Molly's scream still echoed in his ears as he ran toward the blazing light, the memory of the all-consuming terror in her eyes promising to haunt him. But she had to wake up, and there had been no other alternative. If she wouldn't on her own, then she had left him no choice. He watched her fall long enough to see her blink out of his world and enter her own, giving him the reassurance needed to know she was safe.

As the tall grass whipped against his legs, his breathing remained steady despite the speed at which he traveled. The decades of training had conditioned his body to withstand the most rigorous of exertion, leaving him the perfect specimen of endurance. He climbed the final grassy slope, whose top glowed orange from the nightmares that lay on the other side, and when he reached the peak, the stench hit him first, then the sounds, the scene all too familiar. Two packs—fifty Metus—swarmed half the number of Nocturna outside the bordered city of Terra, which loomed tall in the distance. The bright blue-white light of the soldiers' weapons flashed all around him and mixed with the glowing fiery mass of their enemies. The seven-foot-tall forms lumbered forward, their lava skin drooping as if in a constant melting state, and their high-pitched howls never ceased to set Dev's teeth on edge.

As he made his way into the fight, there was a satisfying pop every few seconds as one of his comrades sent a monster born from human hatred bursting apart. Dev's Arcus was retracted and armed within seconds, and he let fly one flaming arrow after the other as he entered the battle. He spun out of the way as a Metus swiped forward with its dripping paw, and then ducked as a mucus ball sped past his head. His body buzzed with the frenzy around him, but his senses picked up every detail. To him the chaos was organized, patterned, and his muscles bent and twisted to meet every need he demanded.

Catching sight of two familiar forms, he stepped to the side of a strawberry-blonde and her tall, curly-haired partner. The three of them danced among themselves to put down the four surrounding monsters.

"How did they approach?" Dev yelled over the noise, smacking away a creature's outreached claw with the edge of his weapon. The parasite hissed.

"No one on the wall saw them coming." Aurora flipped her Arcus around to transform it into a two-barreled gun and aimed down a closely approaching Metus. With a *thunk, thunk,* large bright balls of Navitas shot out and embedded themselves into the Metus's chest. It stumbled back, screaming and clawing at the area that began to fill with blinding light, and then, on one last cry, it popped out of existence. The three of them shielded themselves from the liquid blowback.

"They didn't get picked up on the heat scanners?" Dev frowned as he turned to engage the next threat. *That didn't make sense.* A mass this big couldn't have slipped through.

"No." Ezekial, Aurora's partner, came to stand by his side. "For some reason they couldn't detect them. It was like they just appeared out of nowhere." Though not as large as Dev, what Ezekial lacked in build he more than made up with his lightning-fast reflexes, a formidable opponent to any who challenged him. Which is why, when he quickly made work of the Metus they both faced, Dev felt more than comfortable leaving him and Aurora to handle the remaining two.

As he blocked and attacked his way through the nightmares, searching for Aveline, Dev replayed this new bit of information. Why couldn't the wall patrols detect the Metus from farther out? One or two had been known to roam undetected, but a pack of this size? It was rare for their technology to malfunction, especial the thermal scanners. No, something was off, and he couldn't help wonder if any of it had to do with the recent appearance of the Dreamer.

A growl vibrated beside him, and Dev leaped up and spun in the air, his Arcus whistling with his quick movement, and when he landed in a crouch, the head of a monster rolled next to him before the body, newly decapitated, crumbled away.

"Dev!" Aveline shouted nearby, backing up as she let go of a flaming arrow that found its mark in a charging Metus. "I thought you might be sitting this one out."

"And give you the chance to add more points on the board than me? Never." He settled behind her and allowed the familiarity of her movements to wash over him, each attaching to the other until the decades of being partnered together guided them into a deadly dance. They swayed, twirled, and ducked under one another's arms—a terminating whirlwind. Dev's mind shut down, and he became a purely reactionary being, putting down any enemy that crossed his path. And after what seemed like an endless blur of stabs, splatters, and monstrous screams, they were left panting and wiping sweat from their brows. The surrounding battle had finally dissipated into nothing but a few final sludge-filled bursts as the last remaining Metus either fled or were destroyed.

Dev flicked his Arcus to the side, removing a piece of burning flesh that clung to its length. "Do we know if there were any casualties?" he asked Aveline, glancing around the singed field. Remnants of the battle were still present, from the thick, pungent scent of decay to the weary expressions worn by every nearby Nocturna.

"There were two in the beginning, Liza and Patrick, but I don't know beyond that." Aveline dabbed at a few burns speckling her skin, her blonde hair standing out against the smudges of dirt covering her face.

Dev rubbed his forehead. *Liza and Patrick.* Newly inducted guards. He swallowed back the ache clawing up his throat. They were too young. "You should see the medics when they arrive." He nodded to her welts.

She dropped her hand. "I'll be fine."

"Even so, get that treated," he said and then turned, not allowing a debate.

Twisting a path through the remains of the fallen Metus, Dev tried not to think further about his own recent loss of soldiers, knowing they would be mourned silently, the Terra way. Instead he searched for something that might explain why the creatures were able to move so close to Terra's borders undetected. The thought sent a chill down his spine. What if they had shown up like that near him and Molly? He was a good fighter, but he wasn't that good. Rubbing the worn area on his Arcus strap, he took a moment to look up into the night's sky, watching the endless stream of sleeping minds zipping by. How many were infected with nightmares tonight? How many were adding to their enemy's numbers?

His main solace rested in the fact that Molly was awake now, her mind untouchable. But they wouldn't always get so lucky. And he wondered if that was Terra's plan. Could the energy he knew was churning inside her be used to fight? Defend?

Turning toward the city, Dev caught the approach of the medic vehicles, their sleek chrome bodies designed to camouflage their surroundings. As they hovered to settle beside a few injured Nocturna, their soft hums grew quieter. Sweeping the perimeter, Dev looked for any lingering orange forms in the distance, but all remained dark, undisturbed. Still, his muscles stayed alert, for there was now a truth not even Rae or Aveline could deny—things were changing. The Metus hadn't attacked in packs for decades, a behavior that meant their numbers were growing rapidly.

Shoving a hand into his front pocket, Dev sought out the tiny round object that rested within and began to trace the spiral design over and over with his thumb as his thoughts similarly looped with disquiet. For this change only meant one thing for his land.

A war was coming.

Chapter 8

DEV STRETCHED HIS neck from side to side as he left the Security Council meeting, a dull throb forming at the base of his skull. These regroups had yet to be productive, and he was starting to question the elders' roles in them. They let arguments go on much longer than necessary before stepping in, and when they finally called the Council to a close, had very little to say that was any more enlightening than what the Nocturna Security Forces already surmised was happening in Terra—the Metus numbers were growing and there was indeed a threat of war. The only thing of consequence that happened, in Dev's opinion, was when Elena interrupted him in the middle of sharing his agenda for the meeting. He planned to discuss the Dreamer's recent appearance and her potential to help, but he barely got four words out on the subject before she announced that the elders would speak with him separately in regard to his plans. Of course this earned curious glances from the rest of the Council, which was just what Dev needed—more nosey members watching him. He tried to speak with Elena after the meeting, but besides reassuring him they would have a discussion soon and telling him he needed to keep quiet about Molly until then, he was swept away by her guards. Again, utterly useless.

Stepping out of the Council's chambers and into the large atrium that sat at the center of City Hall, he searched the marble space. The area was packed with government officials rushing to their various destinations and filled with the sound of their overlapping conversations. Even with the clog of bodies, he still seemed to sense her location before his eyes did, and he turned to the left, finding a small familiar figure close to where he last left her. She was dressed in the Nocturna's common black clothing of pants and T-shirt, the tight material accentuating every one of her body's graceful curves, and she had pulled her dark hair back, giving him a clear view of her angular profile. Her gaze was transfixed on the Earth clock by her feet, fluttering as she attempted to take in all the blinking lights. How much was she able to piece together waiting here for him? Knowing her quick mind, Dev was resigned to think it was a great deal.

Quietly approaching, he went to stand beside her. "This is how I know when you'll be here," Dev said, glancing down at the slowly shifting daylight on the map. "If you notice, the eastern part of the United States lies in shadow, meaning it's night there." He pointed to where North America sat under darkness. "The blinking lights represent the number of people either going to sleep or waking up. Blue indicates sleeping and white waking. The number of people asleep is recorded at the top."

They both watched in silence as the counter he indicated quickly shuffled in numbers.

"That's amazing," she said softly. "But why would you want to know how many people are sleeping?"

Dev rubbed his lips together and glanced around. He knew answering her was the one rule not to break, but he was getting nowhere fast by following it. He still didn't know why she had come here or whether the beach was a one-time phenomenon or something she could control. The inaction of the recent meeting was teasing him to take things into his own hands, his conscience balancing on a tipping point between listening to others' orders or his own desires. But who was he kidding? Dev hadn't become Dev by walking a straight line.

With a new plan forming, his pulse skipped faster, and he leaned in. "Every sleeping mind gives energy to this place," he said, focusing back on the map. "We would not exist if you did not exist. You could say we are a form of protection for those who dream. We monitor their sleeping minds, persuading the thoughts they dream to come to fruition in waking life if that idea can serve a larger purpose for the world. And often we take inventions we find in dreams and use them for ourselves. That's why we count the people sleeping. You are all important to us," he finished and stood back, awaiting her reaction.

She blinked up at him, an empty expression in her gaze, and he wondered for a moment if she even heard anything he said. "Molly, what are you thinking?"

"So, what are you?" she asked, her voice calm, eerily so.

"I am Nocturna. *We* are Nocturna." He motioned to his brethren in the vicinity.

"*Nocturna?*" She tested the word.

"Protectors, wardens, watchers of the night, of Dreamers," he explained, still watching her carefully. "Please tell me what you're thinking."

She glanced back to the slowly moving map by their feet. "I'm thinking that I have a lot more questions."

Dev relaxed slightly, more familiar with this version of Molly, and nodded toward the exit. "Come, let's get out of here."

⋅→▧◉ ◉▧←⋅

She sat quietly at the base of the northern tree, and Dev followed to rest by her side. The city of Terra glowed proud in the distance, the only form for miles, its skyscrapers reaching for the sleeping souls flying overhead. Dev watched Molly furtively. Her cheeks were still flushed pink from them traveling the zipline, but otherwise her features were relaxed and her breathing steady. He hoped this continued calm was partly due to him deliberately choosing that form of transportation, for it was an activity that always worked in clearing his head. She proved to be a quick learner. Despite needing a boost to get up on the line, she handled the rest of the flight like a seasoned Terra citizen. He couldn't help wondering if any of this reminded her of her world, if parts felt normal, like home. Or did it remain completely alien? In the shadowed corners of his thoughts, he knew he wanted it to be the former.

Leaning against the tree, Dev took in a steady breath, ready to finish what he had started. "You said you had more questions?"

Molly's bottom lip released from being pinched between her teeth. "So what is this place? Does it have a name?"

"It's called Terra Somniorum. Translated, it means Land of Dreams."

"Terra Somniorum." She tilted her head back to the city. "It's a pretty name."

He smiled. "It is."

"And you said that meeting was about what we saw at the canyon?"

Dev frowned, thinking back to yesterday's events, the soldiers lost. "Yes. The red glow you saw was a horde of Metus. The Metus are parasitic, fear-inducing creatures. At times, they can work their way into someone's dreams and create nightmares. We don't know how long they've been here, probably since the beginning of fear itself. We can only trace them as far back as our most ancient history books allow. We've learned that they're created from the most evil of thoughts and despair in a Dreamer. Demons that haunt a Dreamer in their subconscious are created here, and these demons try to terrorize other sleeping minds so that more of them can spawn. It's a disgusting cycle of evil and fear." He paused, letting her take in his words. "The meeting was called to discuss some things…concerning the horde, but also concerning you."

Her eyes widened. "Me? What about me?"

Dev knew he was going out on a ledge, but he was unable to stop. "Molly, you're so much more than you think you are." She had to be, he thought.

Molly stayed quiet, and he forced himself to look away. He could feel himself becoming reckless, more so than he planned, and he was afraid that whatever he would see in her eyes would bring him to confess everything. Though he set out to push the rules, the duty to his world ran too strong in his veins to disobey any order completely. It felt like an invisible collar in his genetic makeup, and he cursed silently. What would happen to him if she knew? To her? How would the elders even find out? He roved the peaceful land, knowing that was a stupid question. They always knew, always saw.

Realizing he was holding something solid between his fingers, Dev glanced down, startled to find himself twirling the shell. He hadn't remembered taking it out of his pocket. He held in a scoff. His constant need for the thing was getting a bit ridiculous, for it was always with him, giving him a strange sense of peace.

With a blur, Molly's arm snapped forward, reaching for what he held, and Dev jerked back, startled. Not backing down, Molly draped herself over him further. "Come on—what's so important that you have to hide it?" she said teasingly.

For some reason he had a strong need to keep this from her, equating it with stealing a lock of someone's hair—a lot creepy. So with a grunt, he hooked his arm around her small waist and twisted her away, pinning her beneath him. There was no way she was getting that shell. She squirmed to get out of his grip, and the grinding movement paralyzed him from head to toe. *For the love of Terra...* Was she trying to kill him? His breathing became a tornado in his ears, his heartbeat a war drum, and he stared down at her as his body enveloped her whole. When their gazes met, she stilled, suddenly aware of their placement. Every part of her was fitted perfectly against every part of him, and he watched her neck bob with her swallow and her lips part. Their fullness asked to be bit, to be kissed, and his senses flooded with desire. She would be his undoing. He knew if he took a bite, tasted the sweetness that undoubtedly lay within, he would never be his own again. He'd be at the whims of his heart, and the last time he checked, that space was hollow, safely so. Plus, he knew she had another waiting for her, another who claimed part of her heart, the thought of which made his mood turn dark, possessive, something he rarely felt. Swimming with indecision, Dev watched as Molly's eyes dilated, and her face slowly rose to meet his. Just when the heat of her nearness touched his lips, his mind yelled at him to move, and like a cat jumping from water, he was up and off the ground, standing by the tree a secure distance away. His body felt cold with her no longer pressed against it, but he knew it would pass. It had to.

"This isn't a good idea," he said sternly, more to himself.

Molly blinked and with a frown, slowly sat up. Her eyes said it all—they always did—and hurt clouded every inch. "Why?" she asked, her voice small.

"It's just…it's simpler if it didn't." *Safer,* he thought.

She turned away at that, and he felt like such a Metus turd. He had to remember it wasn't her fault, wasn't her past she was fighting, and it's not like he hadn't given her reason enough to want to kiss him. He hesitantly stepped closer. "Molly, let me—"

"It's fine," she cut in.

"No, let me explain." He found himself reaching for her hand.

"Don't." She recoiled with a hiss, and the flicker of hatred, of hurt, that breached the surface of her gaze rocked him back on his heels. This wasn't right. This wasn't how he wanted things to be between them.

The problem was, he didn't know what he wanted.

Before he could attempt to fix any of it though, a tangy scent filled the air, and with a relieving sigh, Molly began to fade, her body a dimming bulb. He moved forward, wishing he could make her stay, but just as their eyes met, she abruptly winked out of existence.

Dev stood, now alone and left staring at the indentation their bodies had collectedly made in the grass. And he was unable to move until every blade bent back, erasing any trace of their embrace.

Chapter 9

THUMP. THUMP. THUMP. His heartbeat ricocheted against his rib cage as he pushed through the apartment door. His mind still tumbled, uncharacteristically, as he worked through everything he just witnessed. Molly in the field, him throwing the rock straight at her, it turning to dust—*her* turning it to dust. All of his *what ifs* verified in that small moment in time.

Now to just show the others.

"Tim!" Dev searched the entrance of his home until he found whom he was looking for. Sitting on the beige couches in the center of the living room, his mentor's brows crept up his graying face as he took in Dev's animated movements, before his attention slid to the left.

"Molly." Tim stood. "To what do we owe the pleasure?"

"Oh, you know"—Molly came to stand next to Dev—"I thought I'd pop in because I had nothing better to dream up."

"Well, I'm glad we were your place of choice." Tim smiled and gestured for her to take a seat.

"No, wait!" Dev blocked her path with a snap of his arm.

"What in all of Terra is the matter with you?" Tim chided.

"You need to see this." Hurrying to the other side of the room, Dev attempted to calm his racing pulse and sooth his mind to the task at hand. She had to be able to do it again. He had to *make* her be able to.

"Dev?" Tim took a hesitant step forward, his eyes narrowing in distrust as he watched Dev retract his Arcus.

"No, Molly," Dev said, catching Molly creeping along the edge of the wall. "Stand where you are." Reaching behind his back, there was a *whoosh* as one of his arrows jumped from his quiver into his hand, a blue flame snapping to life at the tip. Quickly nocking it into place, he aimed down the figure pressed against the far corner, a figure whose eyes now bulged in horror. And Dev almost laughed—for the second time that day, he found himself poised to kill the girl he would do anything to protect.

"Dev!" Two voices shouted in warning as he yelled "Concentrate, Molly" and released the arrow.

It flew fast and true, the center of her chest the inevitable end to its journey, but as he watched its flight, a smile edged along his lips, for just then the room erupted with the overpowering scent of Navitas. She was doing it.

With outstretched arms and a scream on her lips, a ripple burst from Molly's core, warping the space in front of her and sending forth a gust of wind that shook the light fixtures in the room. Shielding his eyes from the brightness, Dev was glued into witnessing a translucent barrier forming around her, a bubble of armor, of protection. And when the arrow met the invisible surface, it sizzled with a cry of failure before swerving to the left and colliding with the wall by her side, leaving Molly perfectly and beautifully untouched.

The aftermath of the blow threw the apartment into a deafening silence, and the air quickly cleared of any signs of energy. Molly slowly pushed herself up from the crouched position she fell into upon impact, and her wide eyes danced between the singed mess behind her and Dev. Her jaw flexed, and her gaze reduced into two stormy slits of fury as they finally settled on him. Her body tensed to attack just as the front door swung open and in walked Aveline.

Her steps faltered to a halt as she took in the spectacle—a half-demolished smoking wall, a ghost-white Tim frozen midlunge toward Dev, and a boiling-mad Molly. Aveline blinked and then blinked again before her arms dropped limply to her sides, and she asked what everyone was probably thinking, "What in all of Terra is going on?!"

⇥⬤ ⬤⇤

The field felt different now, more alive and charged with possibilities. Molly stood fifteen paces away, her hands balled into fists, her lips pressed together warily as she watched him, apparently still put off by his earlier method of proving her abilities. He couldn't necessarily blame her. His actions at the apartment didn't exactly fit with his promise to ensure her safety, even though he tried to convince her otherwise on the walk out here. The problem was, he couldn't really tell her that he pushed her as hard and as fast as he did because he was determined to verify her presence as one that could help fight the Metus. Even *he* knew sharing such information would be clearly disobeying orders, orders that he was already testing the leniency of. So for now he had to settle with staying frustratingly silent again, and somehow prove her capabilities. Maybe then the Vigil elders, along with everyone else, would take her presence in Terra more seriously.

Running his gaze down her form, he marveled that so much power could be held within a single person. Could she sense it flowing within her, swimming in every vein, empowering? He couldn't understand how it didn't alter her behavior, her mind, except to think that maybe such a sensation felt as it always did to her—normal. The thought briefly unsettled him, to be in the presence of such a creature, but he tucked the feeling away, along with all the rest that awakened when she was near.

Crouched in the tall grass, Dev moved his attention away from Molly to the bag by his feet. Ruffling through it, his fingers brushed against a Trapper ball, and he plucked it up. It would do perfectly. "I think we've come to understand that you have some sort of power to manipulate physical objects," Dev began. "You can cause their scientific properties to change or materialize with your thoughts." He stood while palming the round object. "Would you say that accurately describes what you've learned you can do?"

Molly nodded but otherwise remained quiet, her gaze directed to what he held.

"Good," Dev said. "Now I'm going to test your reflexes and creativity by not telling you what this is before I activate it." He displayed the Trapper ball, and its smooth black surface winked under the passing stars.

"Can't we start with the basics...like wax on, wax off?" she asked, shifting slightly.

Despite not understanding how waxing was the basics for anything, Dev still felt the need to reassure her. "Seeing how well you responded to my earlier tests, I think you'll do fine. Plus, this one wouldn't hurt you even if you weren't able to work around it."

"But how do I know what to do? I don't even understand how this...*power* works. What's its purpose? What are its limitations? Stuff like that."

"And we won't know any of that unless we test it, will we?" Dev asked with a wry grin and watched as her shoulders slumped slightly with her apparent defeat. "Okay, let's do this," he said and took a step back while pressing a button on the device in his hand. It came to life with a *whirl*. "Remember to access whatever you felt yourself using last time," he called out and, with no further warning, launched the ball into the air.

Dev heard Molly's breath hitch, and he watched as the ball rose to its full height before abruptly bursting apart, revealing a black net. The mesh object soared toward her, and he stared transfixed as Molly's features puckered with acute concentration a second before the Trapper ignited into violent flames. Quickly and efficiently it burned away, leaving only soot to slap across her face and body.

In all of Terra... She was absolutely incredible!

Riding high with adrenaline, Dev pulled out his Arcus and had two flaming arrows nocked and ready in his hands.

In the distance, Molly paled. "Uh, don't you think you've advanced a bit too soon!?"

"Nope" is all Dev said before pulling the string back and releasing.

The arrows shot forward, two torpedoes locked on to their target, and abruptly the air erupted with another heady scent of Navitas. Almost too quick to see, a translucent barrier enveloped Molly. And just like before, the flaming tips hit up against an invisible wall only to collide with the ground behind her. The land moaned with the impact, shaking free leaves from the nearby tree and rocking Dev unsteadily on his feet.

Slowly the air dissipated back into its normal fragrance of night, and with it Molly's body drooped. Whatever energy she had to quickly manifest to create her protection seemed to take a toll on her physical strength. Her eyes were unfocused as she stared at the ground, and for a moment Dev worried she was hurt, but then she looked up, her gaze coming alive with barely contained wonder, and a heart-stopping grin broke across her face.

"I think you're having too much fun trying to *test* me," she called to him.

Dev held in a laugh. "I wish you could have seen yourself. I could almost see the field you made around your body. It was amazing."

She swayed back on her heels with delight, her complexion flush from exertion, and he had to work hard not to be overtaken by her beauty. She was intoxicating like this, her exuberance brightening the very air around her, and even from this distance it lit a spark in her dark eyes that rivaled the very light of the shooting stars above. Swallowing, Dev forced himself back on the task. "Okay, let's try something else. Can you try to create environments? Like you did that first night with the beach?"

Molly tucked in her chin, a blush quickly growing on her freckled cheeks, and Dev wondered what he had said that caused her such embarrassment. Whatever it was, he couldn't deny the pleasure he felt from evoking such uncharacteristic shyness. Just as he was going to push her on the matter, their gazes locked, and a strange undercurrent of energy reached out to him, momentarily rendering him paralyzed. His head swam as the world around them shifted and warped until, like a flick of a taught string, it snapped back into place, leaving an entirely new scene. Ocean waves hit up onto a shoreline, and a sun burst to life high in the sky, baking the sand beneath their feet. With an excited holler and movements not entirely his own, Dev found himself in front of Molly and lifted her into a hug, eliciting a soft squeak of surprise.

"Do you know how amazing you are?" he asked as he gently placed her back down, the soft grains crunching under their boots. "I don't know why you came here, what wonderful thing brought you here, but my life will never be the same." The words tumbled from his mouth without thought.

Her eyes were like endless pools of night as they stared up at him, all her emotions available to see, ready to be plucked up. He realized with abandonment that his must be just as easily discerned.

"My life will never be the same either," she said, breathless, and his hands tightened around her waist, the closeness of their bodies fully realized. But this time he did nothing to push her away. The honeysuckle fragrance of her skin mingled with the saltiness now permeating the air, and Dev watched with a potent mixture of pain and desire as she moistened her full lips and swallowed. In all of Terra, how would he survive her? Pulling her even closer, Molly's name slipped from him in a desperate plea. He shouldn't do what he would next, shouldn't allow it to happen, for he knew once it did, there was no going back. She would have him, free will and all. And the decades of his careful construction to once again be his own master would be nothing but a shadowed memory. But even with all that swirling, he was helpless to stop himself, and with a determination set in a precarious new direction, he finally did what he wanted to do the very first moment he saw her.

He kissed her.

Molly's body shivered with the contact, an internal wall momentarily falling, and when her lips parted, inviting him in, every ounce of his dwindling composure snapped into a thousand pieces. She tasted like the richest of fruits, her skin softer than the finest market silks, and her body was like fire under his touch. With the sound of her small moan, the world disappeared and gravity was forgotten. Dev was reduced to nothing but a flame of want and need, his intentions purely to claim.

Ripping off the Arcuses strapped to both their backs, he laid them on the warm sand, desperate to find her mouth again. He had thought such desire was forever lost to him, ripped from his hands unjustly, so to have it erupt forth left him quaking with fear and excitement. It made him feel alive deep within his marrow—too good to be true.

Molly's hands raked along his back just as his fingers entwined in her thick hair and dug into the sand around them. He kissed and sucked and licked his way down her graceful neck to her collarbone, and on the sound of her sweet sigh there was an abrupt burst of light, and an energy filled the space. Like a popped bubble, their island rippled away, revealing the soft grass and constant night that had always existed under her illusion. But Dev didn't reacted to the change, too busy exploring the planes of her body, and oh what valleys and dips Molly had. His hands yearned to learn every inch, and they languidly roamed, kneaded, and gently caressed, revering the beauty beneath. His movements seemed to spur Molly into her own transfixion, for her touch was just as desperate, just as demanding, and with an aggravated tug, she tried ripping his shirt off. At her impatience, a soft smile formed on Dev's lips, and he eased off of her, removing it in one pull. The cool night air slapped across his bare skin, attempting to douse the fever burning its way across it. He gazed at Molly strewn on the ground, her ebony hair pooling around her and the delicateness of her limbs spread wide. Unexpectedly, he found himself wondering if she lay like this for the other man in her life, the one he tried hard to avoid thinking about. The blinding spike of jealousy he felt at any mention or indication of this man's existence should have been his first warning that this woman was too dangerous, an already high liability to get involved with. But then she did things like place her soft hands on his abs and smooth them across his chest, which left him dumb and helpless to think of anything but his need for her.

With a grunt he lifted Molly to straddle him, her weight on his lap the only thing that grounded him to this world. Her kiss-swollen lips found his, and her nails raked up his shoulders as he wrapped his arms securely around her small waist. "Molly," he said gruffly. "Molly."

In response she ground herself against him, and his eyes briefly fluttered closed. How would they ever bring themselves to stop?

Just as his thoughts soared, he felt her body stiffen, her fingers stilling in his hair. He inched away and looked into her face, seeing her brows come together with confusion. She glanced around, clearly perplexed, and when her gaze returned to his, an acute anguish filled it. *No*, he thought. *Not now.*

Molly's mouth popped opened with a silent gasp, and she reached for him, but just as he pulled her close, the space between them warped, and she abruptly blinked into nothing—his arms ending up wrapping around himself.

His body instantly cooled with her sudden absence, like a gust of wind tunneling through his chest, emptying the hole that was just beginning to refill. With a pained groan, his head dropped into his hands.

Seconds ticked into minutes and then into hours, Dev not able to find the strength to stand until his duty—the one thing that always forced him to get up and move—brought him to tug back on his shirt and return to the city.

That night, traveling the zipline brought him no pleasure, nor did it help in clearing his head, for he realized darkly that even if Molly didn't want to, she would always end up leaving him.

Chapter 10

HIS PACE WAS quick as he moved through the street, barely keeping himself from running down the clog of pedestrians that always filled City Hall Square. He silently cursed every single one of them, for he was already late, and their lazy saunters did nothing to help that. But it wasn't just the sluggish civilians that accounted for his foul mood—no, it was also the daunting discussion left swirling in his thoughts from the most recent Council gathering. It was almost assured now that a war in Terra was imminent. It was merely a matter of when. This century, Dev thought, had not been kind to their world. It felt as though their numbers had just replenished, when another threat hit, a constant pounding on their fragile populous of life. What was happening to cause such hate and violence to repeat so often? And was it Terra's or Earth's doing? These were the questions that had the gathering dragging on and what left Dev frustrated, because to him the answers didn't matter. Either way, Terra would have to fight first. They always had to. What he did care about, however, was whether a certain someone would be willing, or even able, to help when they did.

"For Terra's sake, Dev, slow down." Aveline chased on his heels. "You'd think we were running towards battle."

Her alabaster profile filled his periphery. "You didn't need to come with me," he said while weaving through another thicket of people.

"And get reamed out by Alex again for splitting up our rounds? No thanks." She grunted as she squeezed through the same group. "As much as I've been enjoying our partnered sabbaticals, they're not worth it. Or have you forgotten how he turns into a spit-talker when he's mad?"

Dev held in a grimace at the memory.

"Yeah, exactly," Aveline said before grabbing hold of his arm. "But seriously, let's not race to our rounds."

"Why? Scared you'd lose?"

She scoffed while releasing him. "Lose *your* dignity for having been beaten by your younger partner, perhaps."

"Considering you can barely keep step with me now, I find that arrogance rather misguided."

"Well"—Aveline raised a sardonic brow—"I did learn from the best."

He laughed at that, something he hadn't done in a long time, and the realization of why brought his features to sober.

Aveline frowned. "What happened?"

He turned to her just as a woman on a skateboard zoomed past, and he held out a hand to keep Aveline from getting hit. "Nothing happened," he said, lowering his arm.

"You've been moody lately." She straightened her shirt that got pinched from his grasp. "That only seems to happen after you've seen *her*."

"I have no idea what you're talking about," Dev said before turning down a side street that led to the closest zipline platform. Sadly, the last person he felt he could confide in about Molly was Aveline. He loved Ave and found it endearing that she displayed such fierce protection for him—a behavior he knowingly mirrored when dealing with the men in her life—but it generally left a gap in confidentiality when it came to matters of the heart. Not that Dev had known this previously, given that when it came to his…more physical female relations, the heart was rarely, if ever, involved.

"Well"—Aveline crossed her arms—"that's an obvious lie."

Dev remained silent as they waited by the building that would deliver them to the platform above. The structure was made out of thick iron bars that crisscrossed and zigzagged all the way to the top, the center hollowed out for the elevator to travel through, and a staircase wound along its exterior. Dev wondered if climbing the twenty floors would be quicker as he took in the cluster of other Nocturna and Vigil waiting close by.

"Fine, don't tell me," Aveline said irritably, "but please stop tapping your foot, and relax. It's not like another patrol will see her if she's waiting. Their shift ended a while ago."

"It's not our people I'm worried about finding her."

"The Metus?" Aveline said and then lowered her voice when a nearby group shot them a curious glance. "But you heard what they said at the Council meeting. Even with their growing numbers, they've only been coming close to the southern part of the city. Anytime we've seen them on our rounds, it's been much farther out then the northern tree. She'll be fine." Aveline stood to the side as the lift finally appeared and a stream of people emptied out. "And even if she did come across one, haven't you been raving on about how she can help?" she asked as they took a spot at the back of the car.

"Yes, but I haven't gotten to any of that with her yet. She doesn't even know what they look like, for Terra's sake." He frustratingly rubbed a hand over his cropped hair. "And from what the Council just reported, they're behavior has been erratic. We can't rely on what we have in the past to hunt them. Who knows what would happen if…" His words puttered out as a chill went through him.

"Oh, then yeah, I'd be worried," Aveline said, and Dev shot her a glare. Her expression quickly fell into a playful smirk, seemingly pleased to finally be on the other side of their provoking banter. Dev was anything *but* amused as he ground his teeth together and clenched and unclenched his hands. Could the elevator take any longer?

"Well, don't give yourself a hernia," Aveline chided. "I was only kidding. If anything, she's probably sitting, thinking of you and dreaming up little heart bubbles to come out of her hands or something." She rolled her eyes. "I even bet three of Elario's éclairs that she's bored out of her mind, safe and sound."

As soon as Dev's feet touched down on the northern wall, he knew something was wrong. He could always smell them before he saw them, and he and Aveline shared a worried look. The thick pungent odor of rot encircled them even from atop the platform, and with his pulse hammering, he took hasty steps forward just as a scream split the air.

"*Molly*," he choked out and rushed the ledge. Sweeping a frantic gaze across the endless field, he immediately locked on to a giant glowing form in the distance. It stood seven feet tall with burning skin dripping and shifting under the starlight, its sole focus on the prey not fifteen paces away. Dev's blood turned to ice as he took in Molly huddled in the tall grass, a mere speck compared to her opponent. Her black-clothed body was hunched, afraid, and Dev knew to any Metus it was the behavior of an easy kill, a quick life to suck dry. It took every ounce of his century of training to not stay paralyzed at the sight and move into action.

But as he transformed his Arcus into a bow, readying to retrieve his arrows, the Metus had already clawed out a piece of its flaming flesh and was pulling back to throw.

"*No!*" Dev shouted just as the fireball hurled forward, all sense of reality lost as he was forced to watch the fate of Molly from a distance. His breathing stopped, as if to prepare his own death that would surely come after hers, but then, like a fissure of energy, there was a distinctive gasp that radiated the land, and Molly's posture straightened as her arms shot forward and rivulets of water abruptly gushed out from each fingertip. Dev's jaw grew slack as he watched the high-pressure blast douse the approaching fireball into nothing, sending the Metus scurrying out of her range.

By the elders...

A frustrated wail brought his attention back to the deformed monster, who was preparing to attack again, but this time Dev was quicker, and without another thought, he had three flaming arrows nocked in his bow. Just as the creature lunged, he released, and they flew deadly true as they pierced the Metus's chest, pushing it back a step and filling it with the blue-white light of the altered Navitas. The nightmare screamed a final curdling cry before it was cut short by bursting apart, bits of burning flesh raining down to cover the ground below.

Dev's panting breaths were loud in his ears as the land settled back into its usual quiet, and his heart felt like it was beating outside his chest as his gaze momentarily locked with Molly's. She stared up at him, eyes wild with fear, shock, and exhaustion. Strings of her hair were plastered against her cheek from sweat, and her usual honey-toned complexion was reduced to nothing but a sickly pallor. A moment passed where everything seemed to stand still as he looked at her, where the stars above paused in flight and the constant breeze fell away, a myriad of emotions flowing between them until she seemed to settle on the same one as him—relief.

Slowly, Molly turned away to study where the nightmare once stood, the blackened grass and creeping odor the only remnants of what just transpired. Dev watched as Molly's posture sagged, her hands coming up to cover her face, and it wasn't until she tipped forward did he realize she was crying.

"Shh, it's okay. It's gone now," Dev spoke softly as he rocked Molly in his arms, the contact of her body slowly thawing the chill that had overtaken him.

"What was that thing?" she asked, sitting up and roughly wiping away the tears on her cheeks.

"*That* was a Metus," he explained. "A creature made of pure fear and evil."

Aveline stepped to their side. "I don't understand what it was doing all the way out here by itself," she said while scanning the field. "Look there!"

Following her pointed hand, Dev took in a cluster of Metus in the distance right before they disappeared into the inky night.

"Colló," Dev cursed. "They had to have seen what Molly can do. We have to tell the Council." He looked back at Molly. "That's where we just were and why I wasn't at the tree earlier. There's something happening…something that hasn't happened in a long time."

Molly pressed her lips together as her brows knitted. The look made him want to hold her again. He had almost lost her tonight—was mere seconds from living a nightmare twice… A feeling of dread slithered through him.

With muscles tensed, he was suddenly desperate to do something, anything, but sit still any longer. He needed to call a Council meeting, needed to get Molly out of here and find Elena, needed someone who might help lessen the responsibilities smothering him when it came to Molly. But just as he thought of handing her over to someone else, he became frantic to never let her go. The conflict only left him more irate. He wasn't this emotional, this erratic in his thoughts. He was purposeful, steady, and sure in his decisions. Molly's presence muddled that. Caused him to doubt what should be important in his life—his duty. What the definition of that even was now, he couldn't answer.

He shook his head. There was one thing clear—she had to leave, if nothing else but for her own safety.

"Can you stand?" he asked.

Molly nodded, and he helped her to her feet. "You're not going to like what I'm about to say," he began, "but I'm going to need you to leave. It's not safe. You have to wake up."

She stiffened. "You're right. I don't like what you have to say."

"*Molly.*" He closed his eyes briefly. *Terra give him strength.*

"I'm coming with you," she said, standing straighter. "I just got attacked by one of those things, for Christ's sake! I think I deserve some answers now. Plus"—her gaze narrowed—"there's no canyon close by for you to push me into this time."

His jaw clenched. "You won't let that go, will you?"

"Let it—" Her face flushed, incredulous. "On what planet would *anyone* let that go?"

This was a waste of time. "It doesn't matter," he said, turning away. "You'll be waking up soon anyway."

"If that's true"—she chased after him—"then just take me with you until then."

He swiveled to face her. "You. Can. Not. Come."

"WHY!?" she yelled, the outburst ricocheting off the wall behind them and echoing back. There was a tense silence as Dev watched her chest rise and fall violently, scarcely able to contain her fury. He hated that all he wanted to do was bring her into his arms, press a kiss to soften the crease between her brows.

He swallowed. What was he doing?

A movement brought his attention to Molly cradling her left arm, and he paled as he took in a patch of skin on her bicep that was red and blistering. How did he miss that? How did he not see she was hurt? He had promised nothing would happen to her, that he would keep her safe—but he didn't, he failed, just like... Instantly he was hit with an anger so white hot that he became momentarily dizzy. "Look at yourself," he bit out, gesturing to her arm. "This is too dangerous for you."

Her nostrils flared. "Whatever happened to me *being the key*? The one *you* said could help out in all of this? Whatever *this* is." She swung her arms angrily.

"She has a point," Aveline chimed in, reminding Dev she was still there.

His gaze darkened but remained trained on Molly. "Stay out of this, Aveline."

"*Fine*," she said curtly, "but I'm going to set up the line. Whatever you're trying to do, do it fast. We need to get out of here."

Dev faced off with Molly, her full lips pursed in defiance.

"I'm going to follow you even if you don't want to take me with you."

Watching the strength slowly building in her gaze briefly exhausted him. He didn't want to fight anymore, especially not with her. Brushing a hand through his hair, he let out a frustrated sigh. "I think this was a mistake."

Upon his words, her eyes flashed with a multitude of emotions, none of which were pleasant, and her grip tightened around her injured arm. "What do you mean?"

"I *mean*, this was a mistake! I should never have gotten you involved. This isn't going to work. Look at your arm! And that was just *one* of them." Each word burned on the way out, but he forced himself to continue. "I said I wouldn't let anything happen to you, and I've already failed at that. This isn't your fight to fight. Wake up, Molly! Go back to where you belong."

"I CAN'T!" she yelled, tears pooling in her eyes, and Dev felt like a man on a tight rope balancing between wanting to do anything he could to ease her pain or land the final blow to send her away, though he knew neither would keep him from a certain fall. "The only reason this is dangerous is because *you're* keeping things from me," Molly said hotly. "If I knew what was going on, knew what 'dark' thing you say is happening, I could be better prepared to help. I may not know how to shoot a bow and arrow, but I've certainly got a few tricks up my sleeve, or did you not see how I took out that fireball?"

He knew she was right. By the elders, did he know! If he were merely allowed to tell her everything, had been allowed to tell her the truth about this place, about him, maybe tonight would have gone differently. But he wasn't and it didn't. All he could do was try to keep it from happening again, and her leaving, giving him some space to think and plan, was the only way he knew how. Terra knew he tried asking nicely, tried to reason with her, but she was too stubborn to see, to understand what was necessary for her own safety. So he was forced to utter his next words.

"Just go home," he said in a low voice, his throat filling with bile. "I don't want you here."

A shallow gasp escaped her, and she stared at Dev as if he'd hit her. But it was Dev who felt like he'd landed the blow. To see the devastation pooling in her eyes broke something deep inside him, so he turned, forcing it out of his view, and walked toward the platform on the wall.

"Dev," she called out, and the anguish in her voice pierced his chest. "God damn it. Look at me!" Her hand grabbed him just as he shot out the grapple hook from his Arcus, attaching it to his destination above. Slowly he turned to gaze down at her, working his features into blithe indifference. He had to let her hate him right now. She needed to want to leave—to give him time to unwrap the rope she had tightly wound around him and make a plan. "Why are you doing this?" she pleaded.

"Do us all a favor, Molly, and wake up."

She visibly flinched at that and blinked back the tears that were working their way down her cheeks. Dev attempted to ignore it all and instead concentrate on the flood of relief he felt the moment the sweet scent of Navitas spun through the air, indicating Molly's time had run out. Her eyes scrunched in concentration, clearly aware of what was happening.

"No." She reached to grab hold of him again, but he pressed the button on his Arcus and flew up, away from the image of Molly's anguish and—right before she disappeared from his world—of her absolute hate.

Chapter II

DEV WAITED FOR Elena to settle behind her desk, barely resisting an eye roll as she smoothed a nonexistent crease from her white dress. The tall glass windows stretched to the ceiling behind her, and the illumination from City Hall Square flooded into her office, creating a soft glow around her blonde hair. He could very easily imagine her standing above them all, watching silently like an ancient gargoyle from her perch.

Taking in a deep breath through his nose, he wished she'd get on with it already. After Molly had left and he'd called another Council meeting, he knew it was only a matter of time before Elena brought him to an abrupt halt during his speaking session. Although it was unlike a Vigil elder to call a private audience with a Nocturna, he didn't have to guess at what their conversation would be about. And it was fine by him—his plan had always been to gain a meeting with her.

"I'm sure you have an idea of why I asked to see you," Elena said as her blue eyes finally met his.

"An idea, yes." Dev leaned casually back in his chair. Though the energy that always seemed to radiate around Elena left most unsettled, Dev was not one to let it show.

"It seems you have learned some things about our visitor," she said, folding her hands atop her chrome desk.

"And I was about to share more of those things, when you cut me off."

"It was for a purpose."

"Which was..."

"Most of the members on the Council should not yet be made aware of Molly and her...talents you've come across."

Dev's gaze was calculating. "How much do you know of the things I've learned?"

"Everything."

The silence that flooded the room was thick, and with their eyes connected, Dev worked hard to keep his expression neutral. Oh, how she annoyed him sometimes, the omniscient beast.

"Most of what I know will be explained later today"—she tilted her head to the side—"when you bring her to me."

Dev's heart sped up. "I'm to bring her to you?" This is what he had wanted, yet he still couldn't help the uneasy feeling trickling down his spine.

She nodded. "You *must* keep quiet until then though. No more talks with Timon and Aveline, and certainly do not share Molly's presence with anyone new."

"But—"

"If you care for her safety, you will do as I ask, Devlin."

That made him bite his tongue. It also made him furious that Elena already knew his weakness for the girl, though it wasn't a surprise. His eyes involuntarily moved to each corner of her white office. How many little spies did she have? And how much of her information came freely? The elders and their elusive ways had never bothered Dev or piqued his interest before, probably because they had never gotten in his way, until now. The fact that Elena could curb his behavior with a mere mention of Molly's name put him at an extreme disadvantage. The paralyzing fear he still felt when he thought of her being so close to that Metus...so near to a nightmarish end...made him simultaneously desperate to ensure her safety and determined to put her out of his mind. The emotional conflict infuriated him.

He was about to agree to Elena's request, when a knock sounded at her door.

"Enter," she instructed right before two Nocturna guards walked in. They bowed low in her presence, the silver buttons on their black uniforms winking under the cool hue of the ceiling lights above. "Sorry to disturb you, ma'am." One guard with copper hair stepped forward. "But there is an urgent matter that General Dev is requested for."

"I am no longer a general," Dev said curtly, annoyed to always find himself needing to remind others. Even though he hadn't quite given up his past duties, a few decades had gone by since resigning the title.

"Thank you, Kade," Elena said to the soldier. "We've just finished."

Dev turned back to her, brows raised. "Have we?" As far as he was concerned, there were many, *many*, more things to discuss.

"Yes," Elena said with a nod. "You'll want to see to this."

"How do you—never mind." He shook his head and glanced to Kade. "What is it?"

"There was an attempted unauthorized entering of the Council meeting today, sir, and then a resisting of arrest."

"Well, have they been apprehended?"

"Yes, sir."

He frowned. "Then why in all of Terra have you come seeking me? There's nothing more I can do about the matter."

The guard straightened at his tone. "She says she won't talk to anyone *but* you, sir. Keeps repeating that you know each other."

Dev's stomach curled in on itself, and his gaze flickered to Elena, who was watching him carefully, before returning to Kade. "Her?" he dared to ask.

"Yes, sir. She says her name is Molly."

⊷═◉ ◉═⊶

His boots echoed down the white corridor with each purposeful stride, his anger a licking flame against the soldiers who led the way, and though they kept their stares straight and expressions neutral, each gave him an extra-wide berth. But Dev could give two Metus droppings about the guards in relation to his wrath, for his thoughts were consumed by the only thing that seemed capable of holding his attention these days—a certain someone who was in Terra when she should be very, *very* awake.

As his muscles coiled with fury, imagining whatever madness she created to bring herself here—for this was assuredly all her own doing, the stubborn creature—Dev also felt the beginnings of a suffocating fear, for whatever it was, it could not have been good.

The soldiers finally stopped at a cell marked A12 that was situated at the back of one of their holding stations, and with the swipe of their wrists the door unlocked with a soft puff of air. Entering behind them, Dev didn't dare look at Molly as she stood from the bench she'd been perched on, for there was no telling what might've flown from his mouth in the presence of the others if he did. Instead he turned immediately to the guards. "Please leave us," he said with a steely calm.

No one moved. The men merely glanced to one another before surveying Molly behind him. "*Now,*" he growled.

At that they jumped into action, swiftly exiting the cell. Closing his eyes, Dev took in one last calming breath before slowly turning to fix his attention onto a blazing brown stare. Molly wore the standard black Nocturna uniform, and her hair fell around her shoulders in a tousled disarray, matching the flushed stain of pink on her freckled cheeks. She looked exhausted, unyielding, and deadly provocable. She was absolutely exquisite.

"What are you doing here?" he asked.

"Hi to you, too." She folded her arms over her chest.

"It's morning where you are," Dev said, barely keeping the quake of anger from his voice, "so I'll ask again. What are you doing here?"

Casually she took a seat on the bench behind her, as if she were lounging in his apartment rather than a prison. "You know I can get out of this cell easily," she said.

Dev considered her, the way her gaze was steady, sure. "Yes, I know."

"What else do you know?"

He ignored her. "How are you here right now?" he asked. "What have you done?" She remained silent, an unsettling look of determination gleaming from her eyes, and Dev became extremely wary of just how far she would go for answers. "Molly, what did you *do*?"

"I took sleeping pills."

"*What*?" He took a step closer, the flash of triumph in her features maddening. "Why would you do that?"

"Why don't *you* tell *me* what's going on?!" she burst out, her hands balling into fists at her side.

"How many did you take?"

"Don't worry about it." She stood and edged to the other side of the small cell.

"*Molly*," Dev said tersely.

"Let's stop with the evasion, *Devlin*." She spun to face him, her hot temper filling the tiny space. "Tell me what's going on. I would never have taken the sleeping pills to get back here if you would just let me know what's happening. Why does this place feel so real? Why can't I stop dreaming of it? And why do I have these powers?"

Molly's breathing was ragged as she waited for his answer, and he was momentarily stunned by the brilliant sight of her, so feral and demanding. Something in him came alive at her challenging gaze, her bold demands. To be in the presence of someone as strong willed as he... In all of Terra, was it possible to be any more attracted to her?

Needing something solid to steady his thoughts, he leaned against the nearby wall. "Inquisitive, aren't you?" he asked—an attempt at levity. She glared at him, obviously not amused. He sighed and spoke the words he meant to merely think. "I should never have brought you into this."

"INTO WHAT!?" She flung her arms out with a frustrated burst of energy, and the lights in the cell flickered and shuddered, as if in reaction to her palpable anger.

Dev pushed off the wall as he glanced up to the panels in the ceiling, then back to her. "Did you just do that?"

"Do what?" she snarled, obviously unaware of what she just provoked.

By the elders, how strong *was* she?

"So, are you going to answer me?" She pushed on. "Or just do what you always do and avoid my questions?"

He watched her pace, an animal caged, and considered everything he was able to make sense of in the small window since her absence. He wanted more time, needed it, but it seemed that neither Molly nor his world was giving him that luxury. Elena, with all her supposed knowledge, didn't end up being as forthright as he had hoped. So he was merely left with his gut reaction to the past twenty-four hours and a fear of repeating a memory that was determined to haunt him to this day.

Resting back on the wall, he landed a steady gaze on Molly. If she wanted an answer, he'd give her the only one he felt certain of in the moment. "After meeting today with the Council, I've come to realize this is too dangerous for you, and there's too much at stake. Especially after I saw you up against one of them."

Her eyes narrowed. "What's too dangerous? The Metus? Are you talking about what happened earlier?" She took a step forward. "I was caught off guard, Dev! If I had known what that thing was,

I could have taken it down. But once again, because *someone* keeps me in the dark, I'm left to my own devices when it comes to this place. And while we're on the topic, why does it really matter? You guys keep telling me it's all just a dream, right? So then what's the big secret?" She paused and raised her eyebrows. But he didn't react, because he couldn't, and he wanted to punch the wall behind him in frustration. By some miracle he remained still, his attention locked with hers as the tension between them mounted.

"You know what I am beginning to think?" she continued as it became clear he wouldn't respond. "I'm beginning to think this is way more than that. This place is *too* real, *too* organized and functional. I looked up the words *Terra Somniorum*, and guess what? It means just what you said, but the funny thing is, I don't *know* Latin, Dev, so how could I imagine a place with that name?" His breathing quickened, a mixture of dread and relief filling him as her findings crept her closer to the truth. "You guys have names for what you are, and a city that you say is fueled by *Dreamers*. Each person here seems to have an occupation and a purpose. You and Aveline go on your so-called *rounds* to protect this place, from what I've gathered. You tell me some things that you deem innocent enough to let me in on but stay close-mouthed about others. If this weren't more than a stupid twenty-four-year-old's dream, I don't think everyone would be so secretive. And you want to know what makes me believe more than ever that this place is more than you're letting on?" Her body came to stand precariously close to his, the intoxicating scent of her skin imploring him to lean forward. "It's the fact that I *don't* dream, Dev. That's right," she said, seeing his eyes flash. "I've never remembered a dream my whole life, and then suddenly, *bam!*"

She slapped her hands together. "I get hit by lightning, and I'm here every night? And I know what excuse you're going to give," she said, stopping him when he opened his mouth. "I've been telling myself the same excuse up until yesterday. You're going to say that the lightning caused me to finally remember my dreams, that it messed up my brain. Well, I have news for you. I just had my follow-up with the hospital, and everything checked out. There's *nothing* wrong with me!"

Her pupils were so dilated with frazzled emotions that they were impossible to discern from her midnight irises, and her chest rose and fell in rapid unison with his—a fan trying to cool burning embers. In her ramble, a lock of hair had fallen across part of her face, and Dev's hand twitched to push it away, his body aching to close the gap between them. Instead, in a shocking moment of contained strength, he found himself leaning away, and the brief space gave him the clarity needed to steer the conversation back on task. There was obviously no resolution to their anger toward each other. All he could do now was carry out the request from Elena.

"Prior to coming here, I was informed that some of my peers want to speak with you. They are called the Vigil. I'm to bring you to them."

She blinked, her mouth gaping in wordless astonishment. "Are you serious right now? Are you really going to *ignore* everything I just said!?" She took staggering steps back as her head shook in disbelief. Pacing to the other side of the cell, she placed a hand on the wall, deep breaths pumping into her lungs in a clear attempt to rein in her outrage. After a moment more, she finally lifted her head, her voice stiff as she asked, "Who are the Vigil, and what do they want to talk about?"

"I honestly don't know what they want," he said, not an ounce pleased by this. "And I'm sure they'll tell you who they are once I bring you to them."

"Well, I'm not going anywhere until you answer my questions. I've had enough of this, Dev! Are you going to do that? Are you going to answer me?"

Why did she have to be so stubborn? Couldn't she see that he couldn't? He was bound, given instructions, rules he had to follow, for his duty was the last shred of a clear path he had to hold on to. He knew his next words might break her, more than the ones he uttered out on the field, but she was forcing him into a corner. "No," he said. "I'm not. At least not yet."

Her stare shifted from fury to utter disappointment, and her eyes brimmed with tears. "I hate you," she whispered.

It was like the world shredded around him and he was left standing in flames, the pain all consuming. He couldn't take it any longer. With hasty steps forward, he reached for her. "Molly," he said, but she swatted him away.

"Don't touch me!" she screamed, and he retreated a step, shocked by her viciousness. His heart raced in panic as he watched her pull at her shirt, as if the material were choking her, and her eyes swept around the cell in havoc.

"What are you doing?" Dev moved closer but kept himself from touching her in the fear of upsetting her further. Something had definitely snapped. She seemed rabid, cagey, and frantic. "I need you to calm down," he said softly. "We need to talk to the Vigil."

"Screw you!" she hissed while recoiling away further. Her attention continued to bounce around the space, as if searching for a way out. Abruptly she stilled, becoming fixated on the single white door in front of her, and a look of relief flooded her features. Dev glanced from the exit back to Molly, a realization prickling along his skin.

You know I can get out of this cell easily.

Her earlier words came back to him just as the sweet scent of Navitas filled the air. *No!* Before he could grab hold of her, she ran forward, and in an instant the space where the door once was emptied, and she ran through it, her form swallowed up by the appearance of the darkened field on the other side.

In all of Terra…she made a portal! With a flash of dread, he realized he was still standing on the prison cell's side. Cursing and calling her name, he quickly attempted to gain the ground he gave up, but just as she turned to face him, the night she stood in abruptly became covered in white, and Dev smacked into something solid. With a groan, he pressed his forehead against the tiny window that was inlayed in the cell's door, now firmly back in place and no longer giving way to the northern field on the outskirts of Terra. He stared into the stark hall on the other side, his ragged breaths fogging the glass.

She was gone.

With a bursting growl, he punched the thick barrier in front of him and then kept punching until a wet slickness turned the white surface red. His chest rose and fell rapidly as he took a step back and stared at the broken skin on his knuckles. The blood trickled a path across his pale hand, and he watched as one, two, three crimson droplets hit the tiled floor.

His world turned upside down, his control nonexistent. The years he diligently worked to create and maintain it were quickly being swept away by the tenuous pull of following his duty over his desire. What he always believed to be true, a guiding force, now felt like a farce, a cage, and looking back at the cell door, he realized with a cold detached fury that he was not a creature created to sit idly behind bars.

Chapter 12

HE MOVED WITH purpose through the thick mass, his muscles only slightly relaxing as he slid into a darkened corner of Vex, allowing his gaze to roam undisturbed over Terra's most notorious underground club. The music was loud and greedy, a beat to distract, and the blinking lights above cut through the hazy cloud of smoke in front of him, highlighting the multicolored neon bands twisting around the black-clad patrons—the contents of the bands was often mixed with the drug Nectus, sending euphoria pumping through each wearer's veins. As the sea of bodies wriggled and slid against one another in unconfined ecstasy, Dev watched with bitter indifference. Even when a particularly luscious short-skirted Nocturna attempted to gain his attention, he merely turned away, unaffected and slightly disgusted. Tonight he did not share in the carefree whims of his brethren, nor did the siren's beat succeed in luring away his worries.

It had been a full day and a half Earth cycle since she had last come, and Dev felt unhinged with worry. He had planned to tell her everything the next time he saw her, rules be damned, and had waited anxiously by the tree for her arrival. But as the hours passed ruthlessly slow awaiting her return, and the time when the sun rose in her world came and went—Molly still not showing—well, the Metus he found after that couldn't have manifested a worse nightmare than his wrath.

What was keeping her? What had happened when she left him standing alone in that room? His body was a tense ball of worry and dread, and he took in a steadying breath. Letting loose his temper here would lead to nothing constructive. So instead he tried to calm his mind by rhythmically twirling the object he always kept with him, tucked away safe in his pocket, and settled back against the padded alcove's bench, impatiently scanning the crowd.

Leave it to him to always be late, Dev thought moodily right before a large shape stepped in front, blocking his view. Dev sat up in relief as the blond form ducked into the seat across from him, the man's already dark complexion deepening under the neon lights, and his long legs taking up the rest of the space in the small alcove.

"I think you could have picked a noisier place to meet," Rae yelled over the music.

Dev leaned in, palming the object he held. "Have you seen her? Is she okay?"

Rae nodded and glanced to the sea of tranced individuals. "From what Becca told me, she is. She stayed with her last night."

Dev frowned. "Then why didn't she show up yester—" He abruptly stopped as his thoughts tumbled with a sudden fear. "Do you think—is her connection gone?"

Rae chewed his bottom lip, a hesitancy in his eyes.

"What? Tell me," Dev demanded.

"Her connection isn't—I mean, I don't believe her connection's gone. I think she didn't fall asleep."

Though not a good thing, it was better than the former. "That sounds like something she'd do," he said with bitter amusement. Leave it to his midnight to figure out how to keep herself from coming here. Dev edged forward on his seat. "You have to find a way to see her. This has gone on too long, Rae. She needs to know about this place."

The music twisted into a new thick beat as his friend regarded him. "Yes," he finally said. "She needs to know."

Dev wasn't sure if he should be thankful or skeptical of his companion's quick agreement. Though Rae had been more than okay to comply with Dev's request to watch over Molly in New York, there was no Vigil or Terra rule being broken that would have kept him from doing so. But this, well, it was going against the highest order of law for his kind. "So you'll help me?"

Rae nodded. "But I have to talk with Elena first."

Dev held in a scoff—he knew it was too easy. "She'll never agree to it." He shook his head. "It's *because* of the elders that Molly has resorted to what she has."

"You don't know what Elena will say. Is she even aware that Molly didn't come here last night?"

"It's Elena. She's *aware* of everything."

"True," Rae said with a humorless half smile, "which is exactly why I need to meet with her. Terra knows, she probably already has her men waiting for me up on the streets."

Dev sat back, knowing Rae was right. Colló, how he knew he was right. This whole situation was maddening. He prayed to every fallen Nocturna that Elena would finally consent to Molly knowing, because if her taking sleeping pills and then evading sleep weren't drastic enough actions to change the elder's mind, he didn't know what would be. Molly was a Dreamer, for Terra's sake. Where was their concern for her well-being?

"I have one question though," Rae said, bringing Dev's attention back to him. "Even if I am allowed to tell Molly about this place, what can I possibly say that will have her believing me that it's real?"

For the first time that day, a smile touched Dev's lips as he held his friend's gaze. "You won't need to say anything," he said. "You'll just need to give her this." And then he lifted his palm, revealing a perfectly round shell.

Chapter 13

His eyes kept going to her, a magnet unable to detach itself from her never-ending pull. A frown marred her features, and her lips clamped in annoyance as she seemed determined to keep her attention on the hall ahead and not look his way. He hid a smirk. Running into Aurora couldn't have been more perfectly timed. Seeing Molly's sting of jealousy, though somewhat dangerous given the fiasco with the ceiling almost falling on them, pleased Dev greatly. He knew it wasn't a mature response, but at the moment he could give two Metus droppings about maturity. Even if Molly didn't want to admit it to herself, watching her glare down Aurora, in Dev's mind, only solidified her feelings for him. And he couldn't have asked for a better sensation after suffering her absence for two days. She was beside him again, close, and he was determined to keep it that way.

Turning down another white corridor that was attached to a side wing of City Hall, they were greeted by two Vigil guards. Their blond forms stood stoic and still outside the room he was ordered to bring the Dreamer to.

"Molly Spero, requested to be seen by Elena," Dev announced. The Vigil gazed at his companion with interest before nodding their approval. Stepping aside, one opened the door, and Dev extended a hand for Molly to enter first. She eyed him dubiously before walking through, and he tucked in a grin. She wasn't aware of it yet, but he was determined to charm the pants off her. Literally, he thought as he lingered over the back of her figure.

Tim and Aveline were already there, Tim sitting at one end of the table that filled the room, and Dev's partner standing protectively by Tim's side. Aveline's face puckered as she regarded Molly, and Dev resisted an eye roll. He didn't entirely understand why she disliked Molly so much, but she would need to get over it, for the last thing he needed was a rift between the two women he cared for.

At the head of the table was Elena, who stood gracefully upon their entrance. "Molly," she said, reaching for the Dreamer's hands, "so happy you could join us. I'm Elena." Behind the elder, a Vigil guard tensed as Elena drew closer, and Dev cocked a brow. Despite her gentle appearance, he was pretty certain she could take them all down with a mere sneeze if she so desired, so for the soldier to show signs of nervousness was interesting indeed. What did he know about Molly that they didn't?

The meeting room's door abruptly swung open, and in strode Rae, instantly making the decent-sized space feel miniature. Finding Molly standing next to Dev, he grinned. "I see you took the hint," he said and brought her in for a half hug.

"Yeah," Molly said, eyeing Rae ruefully. "Thanks for sticking around to explain all that."

He laughed. "I wish I took a picture of your face when I told you this was real. Well, that, and I wish I could have shown you how horrible you looked—"

"Thank you, Rae," Elena interjected with a polite smile. "I think Molly would like us to get started. Our time with her is ticking, as we all know."

"Of course." He shot Molly a wink, which elicited a smile before stepping back.

The familiarity they shared was strange for Dev, and he wasn't quite sure how he felt about it.

"Shall we all sit?" Elena asked, gesturing to the seats, and Dev made sure to pull one out for Molly. She hesitated, still obviously skeptical of his chivalry, before lowering into the chair.

"I'm sure you all are wondering why I have called you together," Elena began once they were settled. "First, I would like to say that none of you are in any sort of trouble." At that, a soft exhale came from Tim, and Dev exchanged a relieved glance with him and Aveline. "Molly, I'm not sure how much you have learned since you've been here, or how much you've come to understand about your capabilities, but I would like you to please inform me of everything you know before we get into the details of why you are here."

She instantly glanced to Dev, seemingly torn with how much would be *too* much to share and what exactly would get him in trouble. Dev wasn't entirely certain himself, so he merely nodded for her to do as Elena wished, and hoped for the best.

Biting her lip, she turned to the elder and began to recount all that she knew—what Dev had told her about Terra, the things she learned she could control with her mind, what she knew about the Vigil, the Nocturna and their duties, and finally, about the Metus and her recent run-in with them. When Molly finished, Dev's eyes went back to Elena, a tense energy filling the air as he waited for her verdict.

To Dev's surprise—and apparently everyone's—the elder smiled. "I have called you all here because each of you now plays a part in what is about to happen. Normally, Nocturna are not involved, but because of the way Molly entered Terra, each of you deserves to know what's going on." Elena paused, letting her words sink in. "There is no easy or correct way to say this, and frankly, I've never had to explain this before in front of such a large group, so please refrain from any comments until I am done." She looked to Dev and the others before returning her attention to Molly. "We've been waiting for you, Molly. You're the Dreamer that has been sent to help us fight the war against the Metus."

The words hung in the air, Dev unable to give them a home, for they certainly couldn't be true. He must have heard her wrong. Elena's version of a terrible joke. Dev sat paralyzed, unblinking, his mind hollowing out as only one thing expanded endlessly to fill it. One thing that tore a gaping hole in the foundation of everything he believed to be true. And it wasn't the elder proclaiming Molly being sent to fight the Metus. No, that he already believed. It was the first thing. The first thing that had his mind scattering, confused, unable to make sense of anything as he silently repeated it over and over and over.

We've been waiting for you.

Chapter 14

THE GRASS RUSTLED under his steps, the night air cool as it danced by on a soft breeze. Dev glanced up at the approaching tree in the distance, its full canopy a dark spot against the stream of stars flying overhead, and with a frown he focused back on the ground, his mind strangely calm for how unsettled he felt. He was definitely still in shock.

To think, he was so hopeful leading Molly to Elena earlier, convinced things would finally get straightened out now that Molly knew Terra was real, that the Vigil would simplify everything. He almost laughed at his naïveté. Instead they revealed a secret so large that he was having trouble fitting it in with the life he always thought to be true. The outrage he, and definitely Tim, felt toward their brethren for keeping such a secret from them for so long—that Rae was a part of it—simply boggled the mind. How much more were they keeping hidden in the dark? And what would the Nocturna do if they ever found out?

"You were rather quiet during that debriefing," Molly said, stepping closer to him, and he looked up, taking in the way her features finally seemed relaxed, almost peaceful under the night sky.

"What was I supposed to say?" he asked with a humorless laugh. "Nothing I wanted to say could have changed the situation."

"What do you mean?"

Dev stopped and turned to her. "Do you think I like the idea of you being this person that has to bear the weight of the world on their shoulders? The whole thing's ridiculous," he said with a frustrated sigh, running a hand through his hair. "When I knew—when I decided that you needed to know about all this, I never intended for you to have to be this heavily involved. I don't want you to be," he finished, watching as her delicate brows furrowed.

"It doesn't seem like any of us have a choice." She gave a weary shrug. And Dev found himself taking a step closer, unable to keep from brushing back a loose hair from her face.

"I know," he said softly before dropping his hand. "I'm an ass for not asking this sooner, but how are you feeling?"

Molly glanced to the distant tree, a swallow bobbing her throat. "I'm freaked out. But doing okay. Considering."

A smile tugged at Dev's lips. "Why am I not surprised? You're tougher than you look."

She snorted a laugh. "I don't know about that."

"No, you are." He inched forward again. "And I think you know it too."

She remained silent, a wariness settling around her as she became unable to hold his gaze. "Molly," Dev said, forcing her to look at him. "I'll be there with you. I'll be there through the whole thing. I'm not going to let anything happen to you."

"You can't promise that." She shook her head.

"No, but I can do everything in my power to try." Her face softened at that, and her midnight gaze sparked with some deeper hidden emotion. He wanted nothing more than to be the one to pry it free, but instead he pushed the conversation in the direction it probably should go. "Have you figured out what you're going to do about getting away for two days?"

"Yeah…I think I'm going to tell people that I still need some rest after the whole lightning fiasco. Say I'm going to my parents'."

"What will you tell your parents you're doing?"

"Uh, I guess I'll tell them I'm going on a trip with Jared or something."

Dev's whole body stiffened. "Jared?" The human's name passed his lips with a forced calm, and he instinctively found himself glancing down to her wrist. "Is this the one that likes to give you presents?"

Molly tucked her chin in and touched the small, hideous bracelet that rested there. Well, *he* thought it was hideous anyway. Aveline seemed to enjoy telling him how pretty she thought the silver band was.

"I guess you could say that." Molly glanced meekly at him. Her behavior had him wondering whom she was feeling guilty toward, and the thought that it could be him gave him the confidence to say his next words.

"Do you love him?"

She blinked. "What?"

"Do you love him?"

"What kind of question is that?"

"A normal kind of question," he said, folding his arms over his chest.

She looked at him pointedly. "I don't think that's a normal kind of question."

He merely shrugged and raised a brow. "Well?"

"*Well*, I'm not going to answer that."

He smirked. "You just did."

"I did not!"

"Yes, you did. If you loved him, you would have easily said so."

Her mouth popped open, and she spluttered to find a response. "So what are you insinuating?"

"That you don't."

"And…"

He leaned in close, his lips hovering mere inches from hers, and he was impressed that she didn't try moving away. "*And*, that's good for me to know."

Molly appeared shocked into silence, which pleased Dev endlessly. He should have probably felt sorry for this Jared guy, that his plans for Molly would not bode well for him, but he didn't. There was no denying that he and Molly's connection ran deeper than a mere folly attraction. When he stood near her, every cell in his body seemed to relax just as they vibrated, their energy calling to one another, something a dimensional barrier couldn't separate. And from the way her eyes glistened under the starlight, her full lips parted on her shallow breathes, and the stain of pink on her cheeks deepened with every second he kept his attention pinned to her, he knew the feelings were mutual. She would be his, he thought, and he would enjoy every moment needed to convince her.

"You know," he began in a smooth voice, "I often think about how sweet your lips tasted against mine."

A soft gasp escaped her. "What a thing to say." She huffed in disgust before stepping back.

"It's true." He followed her with a step forward. "I bet you think about it as well."

"You couldn't be more wrong."

"Really?" His brows rose at the challenge before pulling her tightly against his chest.

"Dev, let go!" She pushed against him, her face growing redder and redder. "You...disgust me," she breathed in a fury.

"I disgust you, do I?" he asked with a smile, enjoying her wriggling in his arms.

"Yes, I can't stand even—"

Dev cut her off with a kiss, and instantly she stilled, her grip on his biceps tightening. Slowly he provoked her mouth to open, to let him brush her tongue with his, and on a sigh she let him. That's when the air around them fizzled with heat and their limbs became nothing but reactions to their desire as they pulled, gripped, and ran touches down every inch of the other. On a moan, Molly pulled him closer like she never wanted him to let go, and he let out a low growl. She tasted just as sweet as he remembered, her lips soft and demanding, and right before the moment he knew he wouldn't be able to turn back, he forced himself away. Placing his forehead against hers, he panted, trying to catch his breath as Molly struggled to do the same.

Eventually he released her and watched with a satisfying grin as she staggered on her feet. "*See*, I don't disgust you in the least."

She blinked up to him, looking momentarily stunned as she took in his blithe expression.

"You dick!" She shoved his chest, her face flushing crimson. "I can't believe I let you kiss me!"

He was about to laugh at her ridiculous attempt to deny her obvious desire for him, when the wind brushed the smell of rot under his nose. His face froze along with his heart, and he whipped his head up, immediately spotting three orange forms in the distance, each transfixed on his and Molly's position. He silently cursed. How did he not see them approach!?

"Molly," Dev said in a forced hush. "I need you to stop yelling and get behind me."

She spluttered and glared daggers at him. "Get behind you? Are you mental? I have every reason to slap you right about now."

"You can slap me all you want *after* you get behind me," he said while tracking the slow, stalking movements of their adversaries. *Three…he could handle three.*

Molly continued to bark at him, and with a frustrated sigh he swung her around himself.

"Ow!" she shouted and was about to step to his side when her movements faltered, finally aware of the threat. "Oh."

Dev rolled his eyes. "Yeah, *oh*," he said and readied for the attack.

Chapter 15

"WHAT SHOULD WE do?" Molly asked in a whisper.

"*We* are going to do nothing." Dev shifted his weight to angle himself in front of her. "You're going to stay where you are while I take care of this."

"Were we not just in the same meeting? Didn't Elena say *I* was the one sent to save all your butts from these things?"

With the sweet mix of Navitas in the air, Dev glanced down to see that Molly had conjured up her Arcus. "Do you even know how to use that for combat?" he asked as she held the device upside down.

"Yeah, of course."

"You're a bad liar," he said dryly as he called an arrow from his quiver, slowly nocking it in place as one of the Metus shifted closer. "You haven't had any training. Once you have, we can reopen this discussion."

"Oh, *can we?*"

Dev was about to give her a derisive glare, when a movement in his periphery had his attention whipping forward. Faster than an intake of air, he released a blazing arrow into the guts of the charging monster. The Navitas quickly filled its cavity, and on a howl it burst apart with a sickly wet pop, sending burning chunks in every direction and erupting the air with its atrocious perfume of rot.

"Oh my *God*"—Molly bent over, coughing—"that's horrible."

"Just another way they can weaken your guard." Dev readied a new arrow, not taking his eyes off the remaining two threats.

They tilted their heads curiously as they clicked in their alien tongue to one another, the sound never ceasing to chill his bones. Nocturna and Vigil still didn't know how cognitive the Metus were, how much they could plan and think, but with each passing year they seemed to advance in some manner. And as if to prove this point, the seven-foot-tall beasts let out a battle wail right before they melted into nothing but fiery liquid puddles.

"Colló!" Dev breathed in a panic as the demons lapped toward them. "Get to the tree!"

Molly turned and ran. "What do you do…when they…do that?" she panted.

"They don't normally do that," he said and, without losing forward momentum, swiveled around to let loose an arrow at one of the gaining blobs. As if it could sense the impending threat, it dodged in the nick of time, and with a hiss the arrow was uselessly extinguished into the empty ground.

Dev groaned. He *really* wasn't in the mood for this right now.

Reaching the tree, Molly turned with a panicked sweeping gaze. "Now what?"

"Climb!" he yelled as he swiftly pressed one of the buttons on his Arcus, preparing to create a Navitas shield. Using one end of his bow, he dragged it through the grass, drawing a glowing ring around them with the tree as the epicenter.

"I don't think climbing will stop them," Molly said as the blistering puddles closed in.

"No, but it will keep you a safe distance away from what I'm about to do."

"What are you about to do?"

He answered her by shooting a flaming arrow into the freshly drawn mark. Like a lit fuse, a tall blaze of Navitas instantly rose to circle them—a protective wall of blue-white fire now endlessly pushed from the ground.

Dev paced the barrier, watching the blurred orange masses on the other side regain their more solid forms. One of the Metus cried in frustration and began to stalk the edge, mirroring Dev's own movements.

"Come on, friends," Dev taunted. "Why don't you step on over?" He readjusted his grip on his Arcus and waited for the monsters to show their next move.

"Dev..." Molly called out behind him, and he turned to see her complexion had turned as pale as milk and her fingers were digging into the tree's trunk as if that were the only thing keeping her standing.

He was quickly at her side. "Are you okay?" he asked, letting her place some of her weight on him while maintaining an eye-line with the Metus.

"I don't know...I feel...I feel really good. *Too* good."

"Um..." Dev frowned, unsure what that even meant. "Okay?"

"I think it's all the Navitas." She gestured to the blazing ring around them. "I don't know how to be around so much. I don't know how to explain it—except that I want it."

"You *want* it?"

"Yes," she said and squeezed her eyes shut. Dev muttered a curse. He hadn't thought about Molly having a reaction to the Navitas, but it made sense. With having such a sensitive connection to the source, of course she'd respond to being near such a high amount of raw energy. He regarded the blue-white fire that encircled them and watched as the tall flames burned like endless torches up toward the sky, reducing their enemies to blurred red splotches on the other side.

"I'd put out the barrier," he said, "but then it would let in the Metus. I need to take care of them first."

The words had barely left his mouth when one of the nightmares boldly leaped over the wall. It nicked its left foot, singing it off, but that didn't stop it from continuing toward them, dragging its leg uselessly behind and leaving a dead grass trail in its wake.

"They're getting braver," Dev said, stepping forward and placing himself between the creature and Molly. "That, or stupider." Slowly he approached the monster, and with an easy swat of his Arcus, knocked away every pathetic attempt it made to hit him with a chunk of its melting flesh. "Molly, don't move from that spot," he instructed as he spun to block another fireball. "Is that all you've got?" Dev goaded. This was serious Nursery play.

"Dev, hurry!" Molly shouted before she yelped. He turned to see the second Metus had slunk to the other side and jumped the barrier.

Clever, he thought. He had been baited and distracted while the other silently advanced on Molly. He should have known something was up from the half-ditched attempt the other made in attacking him. They were definitely getting smarter, and this was very, *very* bad.

Yelling Molly's name, he realized with agonizing frustration that he'd have to kill the one in front of him first before dealing with the second. He begged the elders that he'd do it in time. Swiveling back around, he blocked out the charging howl of the farther creature while dodging the swiping claw of the nearer, and with a twist of his body he sidestepped to be behind it. With lightning-fast reflexes, he sliced through the air with his Arcus and cut the thing's head clear off. He didn't give himself time to watch it burst apart, for he was already turning to seek out Molly.

He saw her backpedaling from the last monster that stalked her. Dev could practically see the thing salivate, and his blood turned to ice as he ran forward. *No, no, no!* He would reach her. He had to. Molly's skin was ashen as she came to an abrupt stop, about to hit up against the Navitas wall, a mouse trapped, and Dev moved to deactivate the barrier, when the ring flamed to extreme heights, momentarily blinding him. Like a vacuum, Molly's body arced forward on a jerk, and the whole circle channeled into her back. Her mouth opened in a silent scream as her hair whipped about, caught in an invisible tornado, and Dev reached forward, desperate to end whatever torment was now happening to her, when the world abruptly tilted, warping forward and then snapping back. In a strange splice of time, Dev saw a glimpse of Molly with white glowing eyes and a tightly wound ball of Navitas floating in her hand right before she lobbed it at the Metus. In the next second he was knocked back by a blast of searing-white light and shimmering red dust.

He groaned as he rolled to his side, his ears ringing while the sickly sweet scent of Navitas and death mixed around him. *What happened?* Sitting up, he peered around the quiet field. Not even the night creatures were making a sound, as if the land were momentarily in shock. Rubbing his bicep that suffered a blow from his fall, his hand suddenly stilled. *Molly!* Staggering to his feet, he swept a gaze over the vicinity, registering a dark form a distance away.

Running forward, he gathered her into his lap. "Molly?" Dev said in a panic, jostling her gently until she opened her eyes, and he exhaled in relief. "Where are you hurt? I don't see any bleeding. Is it internal?" Dev smoothed away the hair plastered against her face and scanned every inch of her with worry. Her cheeks and clothes were brushed with dirt, but otherwise she appeared okay.

Molly's gaze took a moment to focus on him, "So much for trying your hardest to protect me," she rasped out.

Dev blinked before frowning. "You're making a joke right now?"

"It would seem so," she said with a grunt as she tried to sit up. He reluctantly let her.

"Well, I'm not laughing."

"It would seem not."

"How can you joke?"

"How could *you* have played around with killing them? For the love of Terra, Dev! You don't have to worry about impressing me. I'm impressed! I will always be impressed!"

A grin broke across his face.

"*What?*" she asked in a huff.

"There are a few things," he said. "First, you used a Terra phase. Second, you said you'll always be impressed with me." She rolled her eyes, which only made him smile wider. "But seriously, you're okay?"

"Yeah, I think so." She tested the movement of her limbs, and with her ease of flexibility, he relaxed.

"Man," she breathed. "That was crazy."

Dev agreed, taking in the small patches of singed grass surrounding them. "What happened back there?"

"I'm not really sure." Molly gently rubbed at her chest. "As soon as you put the barrier up, all I wanted was to be joined with it. It was weird, like an intense craving. I felt a little out of control." Her eyes became unfocused again, as if she was recalling a recent memory. "But then when I got closer to the wall, something in me snapped. I let go of whatever I was holding on to, and that's when I felt the Navitas enter me."

"I saw that." Dev nodded. "I thought it was hurting you. Then it was like time jumped, and suddenly the Metus burst apart, and we all got blown back."

"Yeah...I...I can't really explain what I did or why it happened. It didn't hurt though. Well, not in a bad way. It just felt...strange, like I was a bystander in my own body and the energy knew more of what to do than I did."

Dev studied her a moment. "Well, hopefully we'll get some answers once you've started your sessions with Elena."

"Yeah, that would be nice." She rubbed her chest again, the weight in her eyes flooding Dev once more with the reality of what happened tonight, what could have happened.

"I'm really glad you're okay," he said softly, placing a hand on her leg. "I didn't think the Metus were a threat once we were behind the Navitas. I would have never...if I knew they could..."

"I know." She covered his hand with hers. "But it all worked out in the end, didn't it?" She gave him a small grin. "Just *don't* do it again."

He let out a relieving laugh. "Never."

For a moment they shared a companionable silence, each smiling at the other, lost in their own private thoughts before Molly seemed to catch herself, and she removed her hand from his.

"You said they haven't turned into those liquid blobs before?" she asked with a clearing of her throat.

Dev leaned on an elbow in the grass. "That definitely isn't their normal style. The last time they got like this was before the war. When their numbers grow, it makes them stronger and sometimes gives them new abilities."

Her eyes went wide. "So every time there's a war with them, you're not completely certain of what you're going up against?"

"It's not as bad as it sounds," he reassured her. "Their ability mutations tend to not be too drastically different from their normal behavior. And once we know their new skill, we can adapt accordingly. If we want to gain anything positive from what just happened, at least we now know one of their new abilities. We'll figure out a better way to attack them in that form."

She snorted. "That's the ultimate glass half-full perspective I've ever heard."

"One of us needs to stay positive." Dev gave her a coy grin.

"And here I thought that role was exclusively Rae's."

"No, I like to think his is more of the court jester but without the juggling skills."

She rocked back with a laugh, and the unreserved sound caused Dev's heart to beat faster. He wanted to always make her laugh like that.

Abruptly she bolted upright. "The piece of paper!"

"What?" Dev asked, watching her fumble with her pockets. "What is it?"

"I never checked to see where I was supposed to meet Rae tomorrow," she said, unfolding a balled-up note in her pants. She squinted as she read whatever was on it and then drew in a shocked breath. She remained still for a moment more before muttering a curse and then breaking into a fit of laughter.

Dev smiled at her odd behavior and inched closer, removing the slip from her fingers. He frowned as he glanced over the paper, none of it making any sense. "What's the Village Portal Bookstore?"

To his chagrin, this question only elicited more laughter, and as he watched her roll on the ground, he knew he wouldn't get any sort of answer anytime soon.

Chapter 16

THE BUILDING WAS unremarkable and small as Dev stood in front, taking in its facade. Nothing unique marked its glass doors. Its lobby—from what could be seen from the sidewalk—was dimly lit and empty save for a potted plant in the corner and a lone elevator bay. It was void of anything that could hint at what was said to lay several stories below ground level or would give away the importance it protected. The only reason Dev noticed it now was because of the summons he received that included the location coordinates.

Holding his Arcus strap, Dev tapped his finger against his chest and glanced around the thinly veiled tree-lined park. The area was still relatively busy even though it was offset from the main plaza of City Hall Square. Civilians hurried by, talking among themselves, and none seemed to look his way or hold any real interest in the building he stood in front of, as if both were shrouded from view. Turning back, he peered at the outpost that, until this moment, he never remembered seeing. And he must have walked this path a million times.

He shook his head. Not only did the Vigil keep this place a secret for centuries, but they were hiding it in plain sight, right under the Nocturnas' noses. It would've been comical if he and his people weren't the butt of the joke. Breathing in deep, he pushed aside his annoyance and entered the lobby.

Calling the elevator, he stood back and waited, for this was as far as his instructions took him. Eventually there was a soft ding, and the doors opened to a brightly lit car and one behemoth of a man. *By the stars*—Dev's gaze traveled up—*and I thought Rae was tall.* The guard was immaculately dressed in the standard Vigil white uniform, the color offsetting his dark skin, and the glinting gold buttons matched his caramel eyes. Even with the Vigil's spotless appearance, the crookedness of his nose gave away the real threat he possessed, for this was someone who, without a doubt, had held his own in a tussle or six.

"Your name?" the giant asked, his deep voice reverberating in the small space.

"Dev."

The man frowned. "I was not briefed on meeting a Dev, only a Devlin."

"Yes…" Dev eyed him questioningly. "That's me. Dev, short for Devlin."

The large Vigil seemed skeptical. "One moment," he said and turned to whisper his current situation into the radio around his wrist. He nodded at whatever was translated back into his earpiece. "You have been cleared to pass."

"You don't say?" Dev raised a facetious brow, but his sarcasm was lost on his new audience. With a sigh he stepped into the awaiting elevator, and as the doors closed, he studied his new companion more closely, taking in the light speckle of gray in his hair and the impressively blank stare that was fixed forward. "So, what do they call you around here?" he asked.

Golden eyes briefly met his. "Alec."

"Defender of men." Dev gave an impressed nod. "They certainly got that one right, considering..."

Alec looked at him, bemused. "Considering what?"

"Your size."

The Vigil straightened at that and faced forward once more. "I'm as big as I need to be."

"Well then," Dev muttered, "you must be pretty needy."

The rest of the ride was uneventful, and Dev was glad to leave the unstimulating compartment, especially after his ears popped more than once on the way down—an indication of the Center's depth. Stretching his jaw to rid the sensation, he followed Alec through an endless maze of hallways. Dev was trained to retrace any step taken, and though he still could now, it was only because of a great amount of effort on his part. This place was massive, a labyrinth, and he wondered if Alec had any special devices loaded into his sensory that enabled him to traverse it with such confidence. Turning down a hall lined with at least twenty doors, Dev's gaze skimmed over the ones that were marked with a glowing lightning bolt—the symbol for Terra and its life source, the Navitas. He was about to ask his guide what was behind them, when the hairs on his neck prickled, and he glanced up.

At the end of the corridor, wrapped all in white and shining brighter than any of her semi-circling guard dogs, stood Elena. She watched them approach with an amused tilt to her lips, which only grew as their eyes met. But Dev was unable to return the pleased expression, still angry at the elder, and all the Vigil for that matter, for keeping such a secret from their brethren. Elena seemed content in explaining away her neglectful behavior of not intervening with Molly sooner by blaming it on her curiosity. She wanted to see why, after all these centuries, a Dreamer would show herself to a Nocturna rather than the Vigil. Her interest seemed more clinical than caring, like they were mere lab rats in a growing hypothesis she was testing, and none of it sat well with Dev.

Elena greeted him in her airy voice. "I trust you found the Containment Center easily."

Dev's lips thinned. "It was hard to miss."

Her eyes danced with silent amusement. "Good," she said and inclined her head for him to walk beside her. Alec filed in with the rest of her men, who trailed behind. "As you can see, I kept my word to show you the Dreamer Containment Center, where Molly will be spending most of her time."

He studied her from the side. "The beginning of more transparency, I hope."

She gave him a small smile but otherwise remained silent as she led them forward. "We keep this facility updated with all the latest technologies and security, as well as house our most advanced Navitas engineers," she explained as they walked by a glass partition showcasing an extensive lab. At least twenty rows of chrome tables were patterned throughout the space, while sleek silver machines and hovering containers floated to and from their programed destinations, mostly where Vigil in white coats diligently worked, undisturbed by the audience peering in. Some quickly tapped away at tablets while others stood manipulating various projected images that spun around the room, moving what looked like molecules to fit with other strands. The scene played out like organized chaos.

"And why are they involved in Molly's training?" he asked.

"We are constantly looking for new ways to advance our skills with the Navitas. The Dreamers are the perfect subject to help test our findings since they have such a fluid connection with the energy," Elena explained. "We've created quite a lot of new equipment since the last one was here. It will be interesting to see which are the most effective."

He frowned. "Will any of it hurt her?"

Elena's blue eyes met his while a beat of silence filled the air. "Molly's safety is our highest priority here," she finally said and pushed them forward. "Come, there's more to show you."

Glancing back into the lab, Dev roamed over the assorted devices as he hesitantly followed, a chill going through him. For as they turned a corner, his view now cut off from the research facility, he realized that Elena hadn't really answered his question.

The tour continued down a few more wings, Dev's mind overflowing with the amount of new information the elder revealed to him. He wondered if this was a diversion tactic, a way for him to lose sight of the concerns he was trying to keep track of. But as they stepped through the combat section and he was given a glimpse into the various training areas and weapon depots—all state of the art—he felt himself relax ever so slightly.

Running a hand over a smooth three-barrel power gun that sat nestled in a row of a dozen more, he knew Molly would at least be protected in one of the most advanced facilities he'd ever come across. He also felt himself growing excited at the prospect of training with her. How strong would she become after the right guidance? How quickly would she surpass him in skill?

"There is much more to see," Elena said as they made their way down a new corridor and came to stop beside a closed door, "but for today, this will be all."

Dev glanced to the glowing lightning bolt that pulsed from its surface. "What's this?"

"This"—Elena gestured to one of her guards—"is where Molly will awaken."

Flashing his wrist to a side panel, the Vigil unlocked the door, and it slid open. A large barren room was revealed beyond. The only things taking up its space were a white table in the center, a sleek monitor attached to one end, and a deactivated portal in the corner.

"Tonight?" Dev asked, unable to tear his attention away from the table in the middle, its size just big enough for a person. His heart picked up pace.

"Yes," Elena confirmed. "Tonight,"

"I will be here," he said. It was not a question.

Elena cocked her head to the side, her eyes seeming to probe for something specific, something that made the edge of her mouth curl up when she found it. "Yes," she finally said, "so you will."

Extending her hand, she gestured for him to enter first, and as Dev stepped over the threshold, he swept the room again before settling back on the table, his body humming with excitement. This was where she would come to him, where it would all start. The future, after so long, finally felt like something he could move toward, something he wanted. That empty space in his chest was beginning to shift. For the first time, he craved to feel whole again. And he knew the one person who could complete him was just a sleep away. Soon the woman who constantly filled his thoughts would fill his vision, at last waking to a world she knew was real, to a man who was.

Keep reading for a peek at chapter one of *The Divide*,
book two in *The Dreamland Series.*

CHAPTER 1

The Divide

THE WORLD IS dark, as it always is, and the sky seems to spin on an axis as millions of shooting stars dance across its abyss. With hands gripped tight, I attempt to race them forward. My eyes tear as cool night air slaps across my face and filters through my hair, sending it flapping out behind me—a flag in the wind. My feet sway left and then right as they dangle above a city of sleepless souls, my body barreling ahead at the whim of a predetermined path set by a zipline. With my heart pounding in my ears and my stomach tightening where my throat should be, I prepare for the rapidly approaching landing. It looms in the distance, getting larger as I shrink, the buildings around me reclaiming their majestic height and returning me to my human one. The glowing bulls-eye in the center of the square platform pulses blue, a beacon telling me to come home, and all too quickly I'm touching down, ending my flight. Retracting my Arcus from the line, my legs wobble for a second, reacquainting themselves with something solid beneath them before they are moving forward again, continuing to follow the man who's been leading the way. He hardly spares me a glance as he nods to the zipline's attendant and descends the stairs to the street. Tucking my

Arcus back into baton shape, I drop it into the quiver strapped to my back and hurry to catch up.

Hitting the street, we follow the soft blue glow emanating from evenly patterned lampposts, my footsteps quiet against the pavement. This, of course, is from no grace of mine—the boots I wear are constructed to muffle sounds.

Gazing from building to building, I take in the strange mixture of old and new in which this section of the city is styled. As if the architects suddenly stopped in their construction, skipped a century of design, and began building again in mostly modern material. Brick facades rest next to smooth white walls, Victorian light fixtures are positioned evenly down concrete sidewalks, and wrought iron fences are placed in front of all-glass buildings. What should probably appear like a hodgepodge of forms surprisingly blends together rather well.

I step to the side as a man on a bicycle passes by, and in the process I almost collide with another on a skateboard, the streets holding their usual constant hum. Straightening my black T-shirt and pants, I resist looking up to what I know will be more civilians careening above on lines, where I just was.

I still can't believe I'm here.

After falling asleep in an alien white room, in the back of a closet, in a spiritual bookstore in New York City (yes, this is all true), I awoke only moments ago in another brightly sterile room.

It's the first time I'm here knowing Terra is indeed real. That everything around me exists in another dimension, not a figment of my imagination or the creation of a dream.

Fiddling with the pockets on my pants, I glance up to another form that greeted me upon my arrival, a man who still walks a few steps ahead. His confident, graceful strides glide silently over our path, and the quiver on his back hardly moves against his broad shoulders as it blends in with the rest of his black attire. As much as I'm enjoying the view from behind, it's the color I know rests in his gaze that I find myself craving. My guide is one of Terra's inhabitants, a Nocturna, and one of the first people I met here. He's part of a race I've learned are the watchers of the Dreamers, the caretakers of our sleeping minds, and so far a person who takes up a large portion of my thoughts, both good and bad.

We haven't spoken since before traveling the ziplines, and I would ask how much longer until our destination, but I'm enjoying the silence. Using this time to reacquaint myself with the city. Something tells me he knew I would need this.

Eventually we turn down a small street and make our way through the entrance of a more modern apartment building, where we quickly ascend a few flights in an elevator. My skin buzzes with each second I stand alone beside him, and I keep myself from being dramatic by thanking God as the doors finally open, granting me a sense of escape.

After a few more steps down a dark hallway, he leads us to an apartment at the end. Pausing, he grasps the door handle and turns to face me, finally giving me what I was hungering for all those minutes ago. With my heart ricocheting in my chest, I look into his unnatural blue eyes and dangerously handsome face, seeing the smile tug at the corner of his mouth. "Welcome home, Molly," Dev says as he pushes open the door.

Everything is the same as the last time I was here. The interior is sparse of any real décor, but simple in off-white and gray coloring, and the familiar large beige couches sit in the lower portion of the living room. The warm light of the fireplace mixes with the cold blue-white of the fixtures around the apartment, fixtures that burn with the energy of the Dreamers, the *Navitas*.

Dev walks toward me while removing the strap across his chest and indicates that I should do the same. "Where are Tim and Aveline?" I ask, handing him my quiver before searching for the roommates who share this space with him.

"Tim is at City Hall, and Aveline is somewhere of equal unimportance, I'm sure," Dev says casually as he places our equipment away.

I'm not exactly positive what Tim is to these two, except a sort of father figure. Aveline is Dev's Nocturna partner. Not in a romantic sense, but his companion in their duties here in Terra. All inhabitants of Terra train for combat, Vigil included, but not every Nocturna decides to become a warrior and guard the land's borders as Dev, Aveline, and Tim do. Others filter into the various duties required in the city, including helping to monitor human dreams to spot potential developments for new technology and advancements in society.

"Let me show you your room." Dev is suddenly by my side and places his hand on my back to guide me forward.

I swallow, forcing away the shivers that threaten to course down my body from the contact. I was hoping something would have changed when I met with Dev again. That a brotherly affection would have taken hold between us once my boyfriend, Jared, and my relationship was more cemented.

I barely hold in a snort from my naivety.

Dev's body next to mine is like being near a giant magnet, specifically one that's annoyingly good looking and radiates confidence, self-composure, and desires that are usually found in dark, dangerous places.

I've never met anyone like him, and all that he is intrigues a part of me I never thought existed. So as happy as I am with Jared, I can't ignore what Dev does to me, though that's exactly what I'm going to try *really* freakin' hard to do.

After passing closed door after closed door—with me wondering if Dev's quarters are nearby—we stop at the end of the hall. I peek into a room much like one I'd expect to find in this apartment—simple and clean. It has the same wooden floors as the rest of the place, a white modern dresser on one end with a circular mirror above, two decent-sized windows on the adjacent walls, which are lined with sheer white drapes, and a plain queen bed resting in the center. There are a few unembellished lamp fixtures around the room, as well as a ceiling light that swirls with the Navitas and casts the area in a low blue glow. It gives off a cold warmth that's surprisingly comforting.

"This is one of our extra bedrooms," Dev explains as I walk in. "Mine is just across the hall." The suggestiveness in his voice isn't lost on me, and I refuse to turn and catch the smile that I know matches his tone.

The thought of Dev so near to where I'll be sleeping has my stomach in a fluster, but I play it off like it's the most unimportant news in the world. "Why do you guys have beds when you don't need to sleep?" I run my hand over the pristine white comforter.

Dev gives me a look like I can't seriously be asking that question. When I stay silent, waiting on his response, his mouth twitches from suppressing a grin. "Beds can be used for things other than sleep."

Oh.

Oh!

I can't help it. I go crimson.

"Don't tell me *you* just use them to sleep?" He raises a brow. "That would be…disappointing to find out. Actually"—he scans my body with no shame—"that would be rather interesting."

I shoot him a glare. "You are disgusting."

"I can be a lot of things, Molly." He leans against the doorframe, the corner of his mouth inching up. "Especially in this room."

Oh Lord.

"Very mature." I eye roll. "Now please, if you're quite done…" I step up and give him a light shove toward the exit "I'd like to have some privacy while I settle in. Let me know when it's time to train."

His smile widens at my annoyance. "I'll be back to bring you down. If you end up taking a nap, try not to dream about me *too* much," he says with a wink before I shut the door in his face, which does nothing to block the sound of his chuckle as he walks away.

If this is how it's going to be the whole time I'm here, I might not make it.

Slouching on the bed, I think about everything that's happened to me up until this point, and how here I sit in a dimension that is connected to my own like the very nerves that run through my body.

I can still see the white room at the spiritual bookstore Rae led me to, the one way to enter Terra where my actual body stays sleeping for days so I can train here uninterrupted. It will be weird returning to my day job. Even when I'm unsure of the things I'll be doing here, I know they will feel much more important than what I do at the marketing firm back on Earth. Well, I don't think anyone can really argue that, given that I'm basically meant to save all mankind from a possible world war. Yeah, a smidgen more important, I'd say. I still have no clue how one Dreamer is meant to make a difference in helping ease the growing number of Metus, which feed off of the corruption of human minds.

Lying back with a sigh, I study the swirling light above my head, my thoughts drifting with the rhythm of the liquid that fills it. Thinking about what lies ahead, I can't help flying back to the past, to the moment of recently closing my eyes in my world and feeling my body shift away, searching for another place.

⋅→═◉ ◉═←⋅

There was much of nothing as I waited in the abyss. I could sense my restlessness to open my eyes and begin, to accept my role as the Dreamer and embark on learning my abilities and powers. But my body resisted, taking forever to catch up with my thoughts and keeping me in blackness.

Eventually the void began to take shape, and I sensed my surroundings—a cool surface against my back, a bright light under my lids, a hand against my own, and the whisper of voices.

Blinking my eyes open, my heart stuttered at the figure before me, and a grin formed on my lips. Constant day-old scruff, buzzed raven hair, and piercing eyes all rested in an otherworldly handsome face hovering above mine.

"Hi," I said after a moment of us staring at the other.

"Hello." He smiled.

"Fancy seeing you here."

Dev raised an eyebrow. "Were you expecting someone else?"

"Actually, I was expecting many someones—oh, you are here." Sitting up, I found Elena, a Vigil and one of Terra's elders, standing at the end of the table I was on. Wrapped all in white, her perfect shoulder-length blonde hair was swept back to reveal her very *not* elderly glowing complexion. Before I knew that Elena was one of the more powerful Vigil—another Terra race that interacts with Dreamers in their awake states as a sort of guardian angel to their destinies—I could tell she was important. She seemed to radiate the power of the sun, making her a force that you desperately wanted to look at but strained your eyes if you did.

"Welcome, once again, to Terra Somniorum, Molly," she said in her authoritative, calm voice.

"Thanks." I turned distractedly to take in the stark white room. It reminded me of the holding cell I found myself being escorted to the time I tried to make my way into a Council meeting unannounced. The similar surroundings allowed me believe we were in, or close to, City Hall—the center of Terra.

"How do you feel?" she asked.

"Fine." I glanced between her and Dev. "Why? Should I be feeling differently?"

"No, fine is perfect. I take it Rae did a proper job of guiding you here?"

"Yes."

Elena nodded contentedly and glanced toward the door a beat before Rae strode in. He let out a small sigh of relief at seeing me and smiled his radiant, sunny smile, teeth white against his dark skin.

"That was fast," he said, brushing his fingers through his tight blond curls.

"Was it?"

"Yeah, you pretty much just closed your eyes in New York when I portaled here."

"She was ready," Elena said, staring at me with her ominous eyes.

"Can you stand?" Dev offered his hand, helping me hop off the table. "This is an interesting sleep ensemble you have on today." He smirked as he appraised my baggy sweatpants and tee.

"I thought it was rather amusing myself," Rae agreed.

I regarded them both peevishly, and without another word quickly brought up the image of the black T-shirt, pants, and boots that are the uniform of the Nocturna.

Surprised, they both stepped back as my clothing rapidly changed shape and settled into what I desired. Elena watched with a spark of intrigue.

"Is that better?" I eyed them sweetly.

Dev was the one who recovered faster. "If only you could change into what *I'm* imagining."

I made a face of disgust as Rae chuckled next to him.

"All right, gentleman," Elena began, "I would like to escort her out and explain a few things before she leaves with you, Dev, and is taken to her quarters."

"I'm not starting my training now?"

"You will, but first I'd like you to rest a little. Much of what we'll be doing today will take a lot out of you, and it would be preferred if you were settled before we began."

"But aren't I technically resting now?"

Elena smiled. "It would also be best if you stopped thinking about your body in New York and thought of your body here as its own."

I nodded, though still not understanding how that would be possible.

The four of us traveled down the white sterile hallways of what Elena explained was the Dreamer Containment Center—a building not far from City Hall that resided mostly underground. Two Vigil guards walked in front and two behind. It was hard not to feel like we were being led through a prison.

Elena stopped in front of a new hallway connecting to the one we were walking through. "Down there is where your physical training will be held. It's fitted with all the material and rooms that are required," Elena explained as she began to move again. "I believe Rae will do your physical lessons today."

I looked to Rae, who shot me a wink.

After making our way down a plethora of nondescript corridors, and losing my sense of direction more than once, we stopped in front of an all-white door with a glowing blue lightning bolt resting in its center. It was a symbol I noticed also decorated the armbands of our fellow Vigil guards and something I'd seen a few Nocturna wear as well. I wondered more than once if it was the emblem of Terra Somniorum.

After a nod from Elena, one Vigil quickly pressed a code into a keypad, and with a huff of air the door retracted into the wall, and she stepped through. As soon as I entered the room, an onslaught of pressure formed in my head, and I shivered. Glancing down, all the hairs on my arms now stood on end, and a strange wave of euphoric energy rushed through me. Something in the air made me want to take in large breaths, like I couldn't get enough of it.

"You okay?" Dev was suddenly by my side.

Glancing at him in a daze, I found myself thinking how small he looked, how fragile—a thought that went against everything I knew Dev to be. But yet I couldn't stop thinking it. Like a shift in eyesight, I could suddenly see through his skin, a strange-colored blood running through his veins, red mixed with glowing white strands of energy. I saw where it entered his heart and felt it beat in my head. I watched his glowing lungs expanding and contracting with each breath. How beautiful it all was, but how simply it could be snuffed out. How easily *I* could snuff it out if I merely wished the energy to stop flowing, for his heart to stop beating.

"Molly?" Dev's concerned voice shook me out of my trance, making the energy I saw so easily flowing through him disappear— my eyesight returned to normal.

What was that?

A hand was pressed lightly against my shoulder, and I spun around, feeling a tug in my core. Elena stood before me, eyes penetrating my own and shifting through thoughts I was unsure belonged to her or me. Whatever she was searching for, she seemed to have found, for her lips pursed and then relaxed. "Interesting."

"What is?" I asked with worry.

"Soon, Molly Spero. We'll get into it all soon," she said quietly and motioned me forward.

Before following Elena, I stole a glance back at Dev, who was regarding me with uncertainty until Rae drew his attention away. Swallowing away that strange moment, I returned my focus to the room, taking in the massive domed space and alabaster square paneling lining its entirety. Searching for the light source, I found none—the room seemed to be lit simply because it wished to be.

As Elena and I walked forward, a shape began to rise and unfold from the center of the room, snapping and shifting to finally settle into a chair you'd find at a dentist's office, except this chair was all sleek and simple in design. It appeared to be wrapped in the soft white material of the sleeping pod I laid in at the bookstore. Despite the presence of that comfortable addition, the object terrified me. What was it for? Was I to lie in that thing? And if so, what was to be done with me in it?

I searched for Dev again, to see him studying our surroundings with narrowed eyes, his expression openly revealing he didn't like this room, which did nothing to help my unease. Rae was off to the side, talking to another Vigil guard.

"Molly," Elena called as she rested her delicate hand on the chair, "this is where you will train with me on using your Navitas as well as accessing the memories of your predecessors."

"I'll have to sit in that thing?"

"Don't worry. It's not as bad as it might appear. You will need to be in this when I give you memories, but we won't need it when we practice with your powers."

I gingerly poked the seat's material. It molded to my fingers effortlessly, just like the white coffin. "How will I receive the memories?" I couldn't help but imagine ancient torture devices and pliers.

"I shall give them to you."

I laughed at her simple reply. "Yes, but *how* will you give them to me? In sandwich form?"

Elena merely smiled politely. "No, I shall send them into your mind."

I balked. "How will you do that?"

"You will see later today—nothing to get worked up over. It's very painless, and you will take to it naturally, as I have already seen."

I frowned. *How has she seen this?*

"All the Dreamers before you have easily taken the memories of their predecessors." Elena answered my unasked question. "This room is where many past Dreamers have come and learned of their history and the power that resides within them. It is specifically made to contain the almost-limitless energy you hold." She stepped forward. "You've felt what I speak of," she said without question, and I slowly nodded. *Is that what I felt when I entered the room?*

"And this is all safe?" Dev asked from behind me.

"Yes, very safe."

"Hunh" was his dubious response as he ran his hand over the material of the chair.

"Come, I have a bit more to show you." Elena ushered us toward the exit.

Before I followed the rest of the group out, I glanced back at the lonely chair in the middle of the room. As if knowing we were leaving, it began to fold itself up and disappear into the ground, leaving the space empty and bare, like it never existed.

I shivered, exiting the room, just as I shivered when entering.

→•■◎ ◎■•←

A knock sounds at my door, and my eyes shoot open, the memories of my earlier moments in Terra fading away. I must have fallen asleep after all. How strange.

"You ready, Molly?" Dev's voice is muffled.

I roll off the bed and straighten my shirt, surprised I don't feel my usually grogginess when waking from a nap. "Yeah, one sec."

Quickly tying my hair in a ponytail, I steal a look in the mirror above the dresser. I hardly recognize myself in my black garb and flushed cheeks. The nerves that flutter inside me are obvious. What am I about to experience? How will it change me? So many questions spin around as I breathe in deep and walk toward the door.

Dev stands in the inky shadows of the hall. Blue eyes like liquid topaz gaze down at me, the indication of his Nocturna night vision apparent with their reflection.

He holds out a quiver and Arcus. "Ready?" His question clearly inquires beyond the obvious.

"Ready." I nod and take the outstretched objects before following him through the dark hall and toward the light.

Acknowledgments

DEV'S STORY ORIGINALLY started out as a bonus chapter I was going to give to my readers for a holiday present. But that quickly became two chapters, and then five. Dev wouldn't let me stop writing his side of the story, and honestly, I didn't want to. I adore this blue-eyed rake of a man. He crept into my mind three years ago and hasn't left me since. So I want to thank Dev (yes, I'm thanking a fictional character—because I can) for sticking with me and providing endless words for me to write.

I also want to thank you, my reader. If it weren't for all of your passion and enthusiasm about our dear dream man, I would never have started down this path to begin with. So thank you, thank you, thank you! Especially my Mellow Misfits. You ladies are my knights in shining book-pages armor. Having you all gives me the courage and excitement to keep doing this.

To Dan, who is convinced I fashioned Dev off of him. I'm still denying it.

And lastly, but most certainly not least, I want to thank Corinna Barsan for always being the first eyes to my work and whose guidance is immeasurable, and Dori Harrell, my fearless editor who makes everything I write much prettier and succinct. I bow to you in gratitude.

About the Author

E. J. MELLOW is a fantasy writer who resides in Brooklyn, NY. When she's not busy moonlighting in the realm of make-believe, she can be found doodling, buried in a book (usually this one), or playing video games.

The Dreamcatcher is a novella companion piece to her contemporary fantasy, *The Dreamland Series*. Book two, *The Divide*, is out now and can be found at all major online retailers.